DEDICATION

This book is dedicated to my inspiration, my sunlight and my reason for being. My daughter.

Being a mother grounded me, inspired me and gave me the patience and strength to put pen to paper and make this dream come true.

Screwed Up Sister

By

Roianne Nedd

It all started at the beginning ....

ACKNOWLEDGMENTS

At last! I exhaled and a tear rolled down my face. I have finished this labour of love. Eight years in the making, almost as long as I have been a mother. A book about the ups and downs of love and loss. I remember scribbling a couple of paragraphs as the opening of the book onto a scrap of paper and filing it away in my bedside drawer. It took me another three years to build the courage to show it to anyone and even then I barely believed that it was good enough to complete.

But I'm lucky I have lots of supportive people around me, people who look out for me, encourage me and inspire me. And it is this group of people who I want to acknowledge.

Mum – A phenomenally strong woman who puts the needs of others before her own time and time again and gave me an amazingly strong work ethic.

Daddy – A man who was quietly supportive and gave me unconditional love in every sense of the word. A man who let me spread my wings and never wavered in his support.

Aunty Patsy – My own personal Lola. Words can't quite capture all she is to me.

Uncle Brian – My real life Adam. My partner in crime and drinking buddy.

My amazing group of **girlfriends**, who cheered me on, demanded more of the book and made me believe that this dream could be a reality. From practical help to encouraging words. I am honoured to have some truly amazing women in my life. Big shout out to Nadean Medford and Tricia Buchanan who got me over the final hurdle!

The Boys – I also have some special male friends who helped me to shape the strong, sensitive male characters in this book. They've listened, given me a male perspective and the conviction to market this as a book for all not just for women.

NO MORE BULLSHIT

I lay staring idly at the spider web on the ceiling; I mentally prepared my shopping list. I needed some of those nice chopped tomatoes, pasta, vinegar, ketchup, yoghurt and some cornflakes, oh yes and... suddenly the urgent moaning in my ear interrupted my thoughts. I had managed to zone completely out of the unsatisfying sexual encounter that I was having with Joseph, my latest lover.

As I returned to earth with a jolt, I had a revelation. I wasn't enjoying this one bit. Here I was laid out on my back making appropriate noises while planning my next trip to the supermarket. Enough was enough. I deserved better. I pushed Joseph off me and hurriedly pulled on my clothes. He looked at me in confusion and asked what was wrong. I looked at him as if seeing him for the first time and said "You're crap in bed" and walked out, leaving him limp dicked, confused and ever so slightly angry.

As I left his house and walked to my car, I had a spring in my step. I felt like a new woman, seeing the world for the first time in Amazing Technicolor instead of the hues of grey, which seemed to have taken over my psyche. And it was at that moment I decided to change my life. In a way I guess I had found my amazing technicoloured dream coat, it was just a shame about Joseph!

So, this story charts all the guys who screwed me over, stole a piece of my rainbow and left me in the dull greyness.

Take this journey with me to find out how I became a "Screwed up Sister".

Zavia

9

ROBBIE

I met Robbie when I was 15; he was everything a girl could dream of, tall, cute and always a wicked twinkle in his eye. Robbie swept me off my feet with his 'treat em mean, keep em keen' attitude. In my innocence, I thought that I was so hot that he wouldn't be able to resist me and somehow I would tame his wayward ways. I convinced myself that he would be different with me. Oh, how wrong I was!

I remember the day we met; it was at an amusement park where I had gone to hang out with my friends. Propping up the gates was the usual group of "bad" boys and at the centre of this gang was the most gorgeous caramel coloured boy I had ever laid my eyes on. He had low cut hair and grey eyes the colour of slate. His tall, lean body was stretched against the gate and the earring he wore in one ear twinkled in the sunlight. As I looked at him, I drank in every detail of him like he was a tasty chocolate milkshake. He, of course, didn't notice me drooling over him as he was slouched against the gate eyeing up every girl who passed. Taking them in from ass to toe.

Once I had my bellyful of his gorgeous features, I nudged my friend Zee and pointed him out to her. Immediately, she told me what a bad boy he was and how he used to date her cousin Tricia until she had caught him with another girl at her own birthday party no less. Her exact words were "That boy makes trouble look like a walk in the park, he is bad news!"

So armed with this stark warning I spent the afternoon trying to put those eyes out of my mind. Zee and I had agreed to try out every ride at the fair and I was game for the challenge. Halfway through the afternoon I was giddy having just come off the spinning wheel so Zee went to get me a drink. I stood leaning under the shade of a large palm tree, enjoying the warmth of the indirect sunlight with my eyes closed when suddenly I felt a hand moving the hair from my face while whispering "I wondered if it was real".

I jumped to the side a little and opened my eyes quickly. There stood my caramel Adonis, Robbie, in the flesh staring at me in a way that made my stomach do little flips. I smiled at him and said, "of course it's real, and who gave you permission to check it for yourself?" He chuckled and calmly said, "I do what I want when I want and to whom I want". The mere sound of his voice was enough to make my spine tingle and the added effect of what he had said almost made me faint. He smiled enigmatically and asked me my name and I swear it took every ounce of my brainpower to remember my name, "Z Zavia" I stammered. "Zavia? Wow, what kind of name is that?" he said with a confused look on his face, "I mean if you don't wanna give a brotha your name it's fine. No need to make shit up" he said while starting to walk away. "No, that really is my name", I said. "I'm named after my dad Xavier, but I needed the female version and the registrar mixed up the spelling so here I am Zavia with a zed!"

He turned and looked at me probably to see if I was making it up. I guess I passed the test because quick as a flash the charm was back on full power. "Well Zavia," he said, "I'm Robbie. I like the look of you. I'll be getting to know you much better. I....."

Before he could finish his sentence, I heard Zee exhale loudly as she barged in front of me with her eyes blazing and her hands on her hips. "Oh please fool, if you think that I'm going to let you have anything to do with my best friend then you are living in an F-A-N-T-A-S-Y." She slowly spelt out the word poking him in the chest with each letter. At first, he looked affronted but then he laughed and said "little girl, I've told your friend already that I do what I want when I want and to whom I want. You're not going to change that, so move out of my way and let me finish my conversation".

Zee grabbed my hand and pulled me away before I could say anything more to him. I was disappointed, but she looked so angry that I followed her wordlessly. We didn't see Robbie or his friends for the rest of the day and I struggled to hide my disappointment. Zee meanwhile, spent every minute telling me stories about how Robbie had pressured girls into having sex, cheated on them, broke their hearts and used and abused them. With all of this negativity ringing in my ears, I decided to go home early after promising Zee that I would have nothing to do with Robbie. I explained that she had interrupted our conversation before we could exchange numbers so there was no chance that we would be in contact.

The next day I was busy baking cupcakes, for a school cake sale, when the phone rang. I answered and was surprised when a male voice asked for me. I tried to sound calm as I said: "Who is this?". "It's Robbie. What are you up to?" said the voice on the other end of the phone. "I'm baking a cake," I said hesitantly, not sure if that was a cool pastime or not. "Hmm, when am I gonna get a chance to taste your cake?" he asked provocatively. "Whenever you want", I said excitedly before figuring out that his words had a double meaning. He laughed and said, "I'm looking forward to it" and I blushed, glad that he couldn't see my face.

We talked for almost an hour that day, finding out about each other. By the end of the conversation, I was smitten and didn't hesitate to agree when he suggested that we keep our conversations secret so that we didn't upset Zee. It never occurred to me that it might be a ploy to ensure that he could talk to as many girls as he wanted, without us finding out about each other.

A week later and I had met Robbie a few times for a quick chat and we had shared a stolen kiss. I was even more smitten. Our meetings were still a secret as he insisted it would be less hassle than upsetting my best friend and I agreed with him.

We were fast approaching the end of the Summer Term and I was looking forward to the annual school fair, which culminated in a party for thirteen to eighteen-year-olds from all over Georgetown. Zee and I had spent weeks deciding on our outfits and we had changed our "perfect" hairstyles at least 10 times in as many weeks. I was excited, expecting this to be my "coming out" event with Robbie, who told me that he would be attending the fair. I assumed that we would go together as we were now boyfriend and girlfriend.

On the morning of the fair, Zee and I went to the hairdressers. As we sat under the large hair dryers with our rollers, I heard a familiar voice to my right. I looked over and saw Robbie talking to one of the other girls getting her hair styled. I pushed my head as far upwards as I could reach so that my face was obscured by the hood of the dryer. I didn't want him to see me with these stupid rollers, which Miss Simone insisted that I use, even though, my hair was naturally curly. I observed him talking to the girl for about ten minutes, laughing and showing those oh so perfect teeth as he smiled widely. Then he kissed her on the cheek before leaving the shop. I think my heart stopped for a split second and I felt nauseous and upset. I wanted to know what was going on. I wished I was brave enough to confront him right there but the combined fear of how he would react and how Zee would react when she figured out what I had been hiding from her kept me silent. I'd have to wait until I got home to call him and get some answers. It seemed like an eternity waiting for my hair to finish and even longer to wait for Zee who had decided at the last minute that she wanted a cut as well.

When I finally walked through my front door, I was a bag of nerves. I made a beeline for the phone, dialling Robbie's number as I walked to my room. Luckily, he was the one who answered the call "Hey baby wassup?" he said to me as he heard my voice. He sounded completely unflustered like everything was normal and for a split second, I wondered whether I had dreamt about him being in the Salon. "Don't baby me", I said. "I saw you at the hair salon earlier, laughing with that girl and kissing her and you have the nerve to ask me wassup?" I could feel myself getting hysterical, so I stopped talking and waited for his response. Then he chuckled and said "baby girl calm down. That girl is my cousin. I noticed her in the shop and as I haven't seen her for a long time, I stopped to say hi. You can ask her if you want.... but be warned that she cannot stand insecure women, so she may be rude to you!"

"Your cousin?" I whispered feeling like an idiot. I was so relieved to hear his simple explanation. "Yeah, my cousin. So if that was all you wanted, I'm gonna get off the phone. I got stuff to do before the fair" and click I heard the insulting sound of the ring tone in my ear.

After the call, I packed my bag and went to Zee's house to get ready for the fair. I had hoped to arrive with Robbie but I couldn't ask him after our argument. As I walked in, I felt dejected but Zee's enthusiasm was contagious. The longer I spent with her, the more it rubbed off on me and I felt a stirring of excitement. Soon we were ready. I wore a short, tan dress with matching cowboy boots and beaded jewellery draped all over me. The dress skimmed my ample butt and cinched in at the waist. My hair was in big loose ringlets and swept off my face with a feathered hair band. Zee wore a short denim jumpsuit with gladiator sandals and bronze jewellery to complete the Roman look. Her new hairstyle showed off her slender neck and her skin was a glowing dark brown from the hot Guyanese sun.

When we walked into the fair, Zee and I made quite an impression. I could feel eyes on us everywhere we went and I noticed quite a few of the guys from school looking our way and nudging each other. I had to admit Zee and I looked stunning and all the effort and planning about our outfits had paid off, but the one person who I really wanted to see was nowhere in sight. Maybe he was on the other side of the grounds, I thought, so I convinced Zee to accompany me to the athletic track under the guise of wanting to check some of the market stalls, but actually, I was hoping to bump into Robbie.

As we crossed the track, I felt someone tapping my shoulder. I turned around with a smile expecting to see Robbie's cute face but instead, there stood JJ one of our school's star basketball players. He was a year ahead of us and I had to admit that he was incredibly handsome. His parents were wealthy and prominent in the Indo-Guyanese social circles. They lived in a big house and I had heard that JJ was the sole heir to a significant amount of land and some mines in the "Interior". Despite all the positive things that JJ had going for him and his broad, dimpled smile, I still felt a stab of disappointment because he wasn't Robbie.

As he smiled at me, he said, "I just wanted to say hi and to ask you for your number. I've noticed you recently and today seemed like a good day to talk to you, especially with you looking so cute". I smiled politely at him and said: "I can't give you my number. I have a boyfriend, but thanks for the compliment and you take care". Zee was following this exchange with interest and she watched open mouthed as I gave JJ the brush off. "C'mon Zee, let's go and close your mouth before a fly goes in it!" I said as I walked away.

Zee scurried after me and breathlessly asked "exactly who this boyfriend was that I had suddenly acquired. The question stopped me in my tracks and I cringed as I remembered that I had been keeping a secret from my best friend for almost two months. I turned and looked at her, took a deep breath and then blurted out that I had been seeing Robbie. I rushed the sentence and said "I know you think he's a bad boy, but he's changed. He really likes me and we're happy together".

She looked at me in complete and utter disbelief tinged with a hint of disappointment. I thought that was hard enough to deal with, but the next words out of her mouth cut through me like a knife "Zavia, we've been friends since nursery. We sat together and played together almost every day for all our lives and not only didn't you trust my judgement, but you also went behind my back for a guy! I can't believe you did this to us. I am so angry and disappointed with you right now. I can't stand by and watch you get hurt. You need to make a choice. It's him or me!" I couldn't believe that she was reacting like this. I told her in no uncertain terms that I would not be choosing and I thought she was very immature. She looked at me angrily and shouted "Well I'll make the choice for you. Find a new best friend!" and flounced away.

I stood there like a fool, in the middle of the athletics track, watching my best friend's back as she walked away from me. I wondered where the hell Robbie was as I was now alone! After about half an hour, they announced that the party was about to start so I headed for the gymnasium which had been decorated and had music pumping out of it. As I walked in I bumped into some girls from our class so I joined their group, happy to chat and dance and get into the party vibe while still looking out for Robbie.

Suddenly I heard a ripple of voices coming from the general direction of the door and saw Michelle, one of the prettiest girls in the school, walking into the party holding Robbie's hand. My mouth went dry and I blinked a few times hoping that it wasn't him but with each blink, my vision of him only got clearer. I moved closer still hoping with each step that I was mistaken. As I inched closer to them, I heard Michelle giggling at something that Robbie was whispering in her ear while he gently stroked her fingers which were intertwined with his.

Each step I took towards them made my heart and feet feel heavy, but I was determined to look him in the eye so that there would be no lies or misunderstandings about what I had seen. Out of the corner of my eyes, I noticed Zee looking at me with a triumphant gleam in her eye. I confidently smiled in her direction but she turned away with a disgusted look o her face, so it seemed I wouldn't have her support in my quest for the truth.

As I stepped in front of Robbie and Michelle, ready to confront him about his two-timing, I slipped on some spilt drink on the floor and landed face down at their feet. When I looked up, Michelle and her friends were sniggering, and Robbie was smirking at me and made no attempt to help me up. Inside I was dying and was grateful when I felt an arm pulling me up and found myself looking at Zee as she tried to pull me to my feet. I looked imploringly at Robbie hoping that he would acknowledge me, even just a slight nod of his head, but he avoided eye contact with me and continued to talk to Michelle and her friends.

Zee ushered me towards the bar. As I stood there trying to smooth my clothes, she looked at me with a shake of her head. "Zee, I'm so sorry that I lied to you. You don't have to say I told you so. I can see what an asshole he is. I'm sorry that I didn't take your word for it when you warned me. I promise I'll never ignore you again." She looked and me and burst out laughing. "I know your crazy ass is gonna ignore me again, but I can't be angry at you considering I just picked you up off the floor. I think that was punishment enough don't you?" I looked at her and laughed too at the absurd picture I must have made on the floor. Though I'll admit my ego was still bruised.

That night I hoped Robbie would call me, but he didn't. The next morning, I waited for my parents to go to church and then dialled his number. When he heard my voice, he didn't even say hi. He asked me why I had embarrassed myself like that in front of his friends. I was livid, "embarrassed myself? That isn't really the issue. What the hell were you doing with Michelle? I thought you were my boyfriend?" "Boyfriend?" he said frostily. "Are you crazy? I don't go out with girls who don't put out. You were just a potential pussy to me and you aren't giving that pussy up anytime soon so I ain't wasting a minute more on your babyish ass." And CLICK that bastard had just had the nerve to put the phone down on me. I redialed but he wouldn't answer and I was stuck brooding over him for the rest of the day. Over the next week, I tried to call him back a few times but he never answered or disconnected my calls and finally, I stopped calling for my own sanity.

JJ

Two weeks after the Robbie incident I bumped into JJ. Zee and I were in Demico, our favourite ice cream parlour. We ordered crepes and as usual, Zee wanted extra sugar so left me at the table to get some. I was facing the window trying to fix my fringe and hoping that no one noticed me when there on the other side of the window was JJ smiling and waving at me. I smiled back and waved feeling mortified. As Zee came back, I gladly turned away and we started to eat. I looked up from my plate to see Zee looking up, and beckoning for someone to come over. Next thing you know, JJ was sitting next to Zee and opposite me beaming. "Hello again", he said. "Hi", I replied wondering when Zee had become so friendly with JJ.

Zee then pushed her plate away, wiped her mouth and conveniently remembered that she had somewhere else to be. She excused herself and told JJ to finish her crepes. I tried to catch her eye but she avoided my glare and ducked out of the door. JJ and I sat in uncomfortable silence, eating and avoiding eye contact. Then finally he said to me "you know Zavia, I've wanted to talk to you properly for a long time but because Adam is my teammate I had to think long and hard about whether it would be a good move because everyone knows he is protective of his little sister." "Little sister?" I spluttered. "JJ he is only ten months older than me and we are in the same class at school. I hardly think that I am his little sister". "Well that's what he calls you, so I was worried about asking you out. Then at the fair, I plucked up the courage to talk to you but you were caught up with Robbie!", I was so mortified, I couldn't respond so I kept eating with my head down.

But then JJ took my hand and asked me to look at him and said "Zavia I wasn't laughing at you or judging you. I wanted to give you your space before I tried again. You're so beautiful. I wanted you to know that I'm interested in you. I'd love for us to go on a date". I was taken aback and more than a little flattered. So with a smile and a nod, I said, "I'd like that too".

For the next six months, I dated JJ. I spent lots of time watching him play basketball and we would take long walks together and talk about our shared interests. We spent all our

19

free time together which annoyed Zee, who thought I was way too into him. It also annoyed Adam because it meant I was in his space a lot more too. But I didn't care I was smitten.

As we approached my 16th birthday party, I asked JJ to be my date. It was perfect, we wore matching outfits and swayed the night away. As we danced, I whispered to him that I wished the night would never end and he murmured "I know what you mean baby. Soon we can have that never-ending night. After all, you're legal now". I smiled thinking I might be legal in the eyes of the law, but all night parties were definitely not part of the rules in my house.

A couple of weeks after my birthday, JJ said that he had a late birthday surprise for me, I just need to be available for a whole afternoon. We arranged to meet at his house and on my way there I could barely contain my surprise as I couldn't imagine what he had in store for me. When I got there, his parents weren't home but I heard lots of noise from upstairs so I assumed that his brothers were home watching basketball. He suggested we sit downstairs in the lounge. As I walked in, I smiled when I saw a stack of films waiting to be watched and a rug on the floor for us to snuggle. "This is really romantic", I said dreamily as I sank down to sit on the rug as he set up the first film.

Halfway through the film, he kissed me and as we kissed, I felt an urgency emanating from him that I didn't remember ever experiencing before. His hands were on my thighs and next thing I knew he had unzipped my jeans and was trying to push his hand into them. I tried to slow him down but he was intent on pulling at my panties and raggedly whispered "lace! I like that".

I asked him to stop and tried to get up but as I tried to stand he used the opportunity to pull my jeans with more force. I fell back, giving him the chance to get on top of me. "Calm down", he said. "You know you want this. Don't worry, you're legal now. I'm just sorry it's not a whole night like I promised". With horrifying clarity, I now understood what he had meant on my 16th birthday but I still said: "What are you talking about?" "Your birthday, Honey. You're legal now." He replied "I didn't know you meant this" I said. "I thought you meant partying all night." "Oh please! Don't pretend to be so innocent. You knew what I meant."

Seeing how determined he was becoming scared me. I tried to push him off me. We started to fight, but I was pressed against the sofa. He was determined to pull off my jeans and I was determined to keep them on. This went on for what felt like an eternity. He was getting more aggressive saying "just take the fucking jeans off. What is your problem? I bet Robbie didn't have to work so hard!" "Robbie?" I said. "What the fuck does Robbie have to do with this?" We all know you slept with Robbie. Why can't I at least get some of that action? At least I gave you a break and waited until you were off age!" He snarled. "I didn't do shit with Robbie", I said. "I swear I didn't. I'm a virgin. Please stop?" I pleaded.   I felt so hurt, JJ had changed. I couldn't believe the nightmare that I was in, but I was determined not to lose my jeans.

As we tussled, I elbowed JJ in the face and took the opportunity to roll away from him. I was up and running towards the lounge door as fast as my legs could carry me while pulling my jeans up to my waist properly. But he was faster than me and grabbed me attempting to drag me back through the doorway. I screamed and he tried to cover my mouth. He told me to shut up, but I kept screaming hoping that the sound would carry far enough for someone to hear me. The TV went quiet and a male voice said: "Can you hear screaming?" Someone said yes and I listened to what sounded like a herd of elephants moving around and then I heard many feet thundering down the stairs.

As they came into view, I saw that many of JJ's teammates were at the house as well. Then I saw them. A pair of brown eyes identical to mine and I almost fainted. My brother Adam was there and had been watching basketball upstairs. When he saw me and noticed JJ's hands roughly clenched around my arm, he went crazy. As if in slow motion he pushed past the other boys. When he got to JJ, he grabbed him by the neck and screamed "What the fuck are you trying to do to my sister? Answer me you little cunt. I said why the fuck is my sister in your house screaming like her fucking life depends on it? You

21

had better fucking answer me before I make you cry like a bitch" It took five of the boys to yank him off while I pleaded with him to take me home and JJ kept repeating "ask her, ask her".

Finally, I managed to drag him out of the house and to his car. He got into the driver seat still huffing and puffing. For the duration of the ride home, he muttered about wanting to kill JJ and calling me stupid. I wordlessly stared out of the window and was glad when he dropped me off at home before going for a drive to clear his head. I went into the house, straight to bed and lay there shaking. Try as I might I couldn't stop replaying the afternoon in my mind. I only stopped when I fell into a fitful sleep. The next thing I knew there was sun streaming into my room and my little sister, Joanna or JoJo, as she is affectionately known, was knocking at my bedroom door insistently saying that I had a phone call. I mumbled, "come in" and took the phone that she placed in my outstretched hand.

I couldn't believe someone was calling my house so early. "Yes Zee", I said groggily assuming that it was Zee. JoJo giggled and said with an air of drama "it isn't Zee, it's a boy". As she skipped out laughing, I heard an angry voice saying "it's not Zee, its JJ". I rolled my eyes and said "yes". "I just wanted you to know that if you want to continue dating me and ever step foot in my house again, you either suck it or fuck it but either way you owe me!" I put the phone down and wondered what the hell I was going to do to get out of this with some pride intact.

There was only one option, I needed to talk to Zee and come up with a plan! As soon as it felt late enough to phone Zee's house I punched in her number and was grateful when she answered. "We need to talk", I said. "I need a way to get rid of JJ." " OOOOh why?" she said. "You know I like a bit of drama. Let's meet at Demico at lunchtime."

When I got to Demico, Zee was standing outside waiting. I grabbed her hand and we went in. Once we had ordered an ice cream sundae to share, I told her all about how JJ had almost deflowered me on an old rug in his parents' lounge. As

I described how Adam had attacked JJ, she looked at me in shock and said "whoa Zavia you really know how to lead an exciting life" and she chuckled.

"It isn't funny Zee. What am I going to do? I really like JJ, but I don't want to have sex yet. He scared me with how aggressive he behaved." "Honestly, Zavia you have no option. Liking him is not enough. He treated you badly and you need to break it off with him." "Ok", I sighed. "How should I do it?" I said. "Well", she replied, "there's a big basketball game on Friday evening. I suggest that you do it publicly." "Ok", I said, "how, though?" "Leave it to me", she said. "Make sure you look hot on Friday as well." "Cool", I said, "that shouldn't be too hard".

The week felt like the longest week ever and Friday dragged by because I was anxious to go home and get ready for the game. My eldest sister Lola was home with her husband Tyrone for a vacation so offered to help me do my hair and nails. I was wearing a pair of shorts and a basketball vest that Tyrone had brought for me from the States. I wore mini basketball earrings and a pair of red and black Jordan's. I was meeting Zee at her house and then her father would drive us to the Sports Hall.

At Zee's house, I was amused to see that she had on purple and yellow in homage to her favourite team the LA Lakers. She was wearing a basketball vest as well, but she had fashioned hers into a mini dress. I was slightly envious of her ability to make clothes and customise outfits at the drop of a hat. "You ready for this?" she said. "Yea, best to get it over with. I just want to get out of it with my reputation intact." "I've got your back Zav, don't worry", she said and as usual, I trusted her implicitly.

When we got to the Sports Hall, we sat directly behind the hoop which our school would be shooting towards. As I was Adam's sister and he was a star player we got great seats. As we put our bags down Zee said: "I'm just going to get us some drinks and stuff, hold my place". "Cool, will do", I said. A couple of minutes after Zee disappeared, some older guys who had left our school the year before came up onto the bleachers and sat directly behind me. One of them was very cute, I remembered his face but not his name. His green eyes gave away his Portuguese heritage and his curly blond/brown hair was just delicious. "Hey", he said. "Have you seen Zayasha?" "Yes", I said surprised that he knew Zee and always surprised when someone referred to her by her full name, Zayasha, which she hardly used. "She asked me to meet her here at the game with a couple of my buddies" he explained. "Oh, she's just gone to get us some drinks", I said politely wondering what was going on. "So I guess that you're Zavia?" he said interrupting my thoughts. I nodded at him and he said "nice to meet you. I'm Reece. Zayasha has told me a lot about you". "Oh did she now?" I said turning to face him. "Yea, she said that you had a problem and she asked me to help out" "How are you going to help?" I said. "Move down and I'll show you" he replied with a mischievous look in his sparkling green eyes.

I'm not sure why I went along with it, but I moved down as he asked. He climbed over the bleacher so he was sitting in what had been Zee's space and slung his arm around me whispering softly in my ear "just go along with it. It's all part of the plan". He explained that he intended to flirt with me all night and make everyone think that we were an item. This would send a clear message to JJ that I was done with him. Meanwhile, Zee was spreading the rumour that I had dumped him for an older guy so any retaliation from him would seem like the ranting of a jealous and bitter ex. It was a perfect scheme. "O.K I'm in", I said thinking that Zee was a genius. "But one question. What's in it for you?" "It's a favour to my boy, Gerald. He wants to hook up with Zayasha and me doing this will earn him some pussy points that hopefully he can cash in with her later tonight." I blushed and he said "Wow, are you seriously blushing? Zayasha told me that you weren't as open as she is but I didn't believe her. How can you two be so close, yet so different?" "Different how?" I enquired. "Well, Zayasha is foxy and in your face and you... Well, you seem so innocent. Almost virginal" he said thoughtfully. I laughed and said, "Virginal seems a little extreme but I have much stricter parents so that probably has a lot to do with it". "Guess so", he replied. "Anyway, let the games begin", he said as he moved his hand up my back and rubbed my neck. I flinched at first but it felt good and he moved closer and said: "Hey relax, we may as well enjoy it hadn't we?"

By halftime, JJ had definitely noticed. Some of his friends were sitting near Reece and I and had apparently gone courtside to report my perceived indiscretion to him. Reece was very attentive. We talked and joked and I was surprised to find that it felt like we had known each other for years. Zee's plan was working better than we imagined. JJ was throwing dirty looks our way and each time, Reece smiled and waved at him and I giggled. As the game ended I turned to ask Zee if she was ready to go but Reece said, "I don't mind taking you home Zavia. I think Zayasha probably has things to do". As he said it, he looked at Gerald meaningfully and I blushed again knowing I would hear all the details from Zee the next day. "Are you sure you don't mind taking me home? I may need you to take my brother Adam too if it's not too much to ask." I said hesitantly. "No, it's fine", he said. "Why don't you run down and check with him? And I'll meet you at the door". "Great", I said. I bounded down the bleachers to see if Adam wanted a ride but he declined as he was going out with his friends to celebrate their victory. I told him goodbye and made my way to the door.

When I got to the doors, I saw Reece. I smiled at him and asked him again "Are you sure this is ok? I don't want to be any bother and it seems like you've done enough for me tonight already". "It's cool," he said, "It's my pleasure". "Thanks", I said gratefully while scanning the crowd to see if Zee had already left. I spotted her ahead of us and we hurried to catch them up. Zee barely noticed us she had an indescribable look on her face and was totally engrossed in Gerald, who had his arm around her. We walked with them until we reached Gerald's car and then said our goodbyes.

As Reece and I walked further into the car park, he pointed out his car on the other side of the lot. We made our way over to it weaving through the crowd and around cars. I bumped into someone nearly falling and Reece grabbed my arm to steady me. As it was so busy, he continued holding me and guiding me through the crowd with his body pressed lightly against mine. When we had almost reached the car, we heard someone shout "Yo!" I kept walking assuming that the call was for someone else. "Yo, Zavia!" the person yelled. Reece and I stopped and I turned to see JJ with some of his friends walking towards me. "Oh here we go", I murmured, "let's keep walking Reece". We resumed walking and Reece reached out and took my hand. Then I heard running behind us and felt rather than saw JJ shove Reece from behind. Reece turned around quickly and said "yo bro what the fuck?" while adopting an aggressive stance with me tucked behind him. "Yea what the fuck indeed? You're here with my girl and expect me to take it lying down? You're way disrespectful man." JJ spat out through gritted teeth. "From what I heard, the only disrespectful person around here is you, little boy", said Reece angrily. "Let's just go", I said to Reece, worried that things might get out of hand. "JJ leave us alone. I don't want to be with you anymore. I'm not your girl", I said emphatically. "I don't want any trouble." "Ha! That's all you are. A whole load of trouble. You're a little prick tease. Does big man here know that you don't put out?" JJ shouted angrily. Before I could reply, Reece responded by saying "Big man knows everything about Zavia and I like it all. So why don't you just back the fuck up and leave us alone?" JJ shook his head in disgust and said: "Whatever man, this bitch owes me a fuck and I will be collecting it from her at some point".

Without warning, Reece punched JJ straight in the face and said "don't you have any respect for women? Don't you have a mother? Who da fuck are you calling a bitch? Cut that shit out. First, you push me and then you wanna be calling Zavia names? Let me be clear. If you ever touch her again, you will be dealing with me and mine". JJ stood there rubbing his jaw, looking from me to Reece and back and then said: "she ain't even worth all this hassle, I'm out". Reece stood staring at him belligerently as he retreated and I stared at Reece not knowing what to say, do or think. "Come on Zavia", he said. "Let's get you home." "I'm really sorry Reece. I didn't mean to get you so involved." "It's cool", he said. "I have a sister and female cousins. I know what guys can be like sometimes. You seem like a genuinely sweet girl so it was my pleasure to defend your honour." "Thanks", I said. We had reached his car and he opened the door for me. He was a real gentleman. He drove directly to my house with no suggestive comments about taking a detour and when we stopped, he told me that he'd had a great evening and wouldn't mind seeing me again soon. I thanked him and said, "I'd like to see you again too".

As I walked up the steps, my mother opened the door and Reece tooted his horn and drove off. "Who was that Zavia?" she asked. "It was Reece Rodrigues mum. He's a friend of Zayasha's." "Oh ok", she said. "I went to school with some Rodrigues. Who is his dad?" "I think his dad is Paul Rodrigues Mum. The one who owns the hotel on the East Coast." "Oh yes, I know Paul and his sisters. They're a well-connected family. Full of girls if I remember rightly. Finally, you seem to be keeping the right company." I rolled my eyes and skipped up the stairs before she could give me one of her lectures about the haves and have-nots within Guyanese Society.

REECE

"Zavia, Zavia", Zee's voice permeated my consciousness and I could feel her shaking me out of my sleep. "What?" I said groggily, thinking that having my sleep interrupted was becoming a habit. I opened my eyes and saw her sitting next to me on my bed. "For goodness sake, wake up Zavia", she said. "Why" I mumbled. "Because it's Saturday and we have stuff we could be doing. There's a craft class in town that I wanted to check out and you promised to help me plait my hair. I'm also supposed to go to my granny's party this evening. Do you want to come?" I rubbed my eyes and said, "exactly what time is it?" "8am", she said. "Oh Zee" I groaned "why, why, why? I wish you could have left it until at least 9am. Why did my mum even allow you into the house at this time?" "Well, you're lucky I wasn't here at 7am. My mum has a new yoga regime so she woke me up at 6am with all her noise. It took self-control not to run over here at like 6.30am to fill you in on the details of last night. Oh and, of course, your mum let me in. She thinks I'm a good influence on you with all these early starts."

I sniggered and said, "if my mum only knew the real you Zee". She playfully pulled my hair and stuck her tongue out. "If you're going to be horrible, I won't tell you about Gerald", she said. "Ok, I take it all back. Tell me what happened". "It was incredible," she said dramatically. "His brother has an apartment in Kitty so we went there after the game. We had it to ourselves because his brother is away. He had set it all up with lots of candles. He even had a mixed tape ready. He poured us some drinks and we kissed and kissed for what seemed like ages. Then he told me that he wanted to do something special. He took me into the bedroom and undressed me slowly. I thought I was going to faint with anticipation. It was so different to that idiot Gavin who couldn't even hold it together to get my clothes off." I laughed and said, "yes I remember Gavin, but right now I want to hear more about Gerald". "Aaah yes the delectable Gerald." She said dreamily. "Once I was naked, he lay me on the bed and then he sucked my toes." "Ewww", I said, disgusted t the thought. "No, no it's nice", she said defensively. "It sounds horrible, but it felt exquisite," she said pausing to presumably savour the moment.

"Then he moved up slowly. Trailing my body with kisses. I thought it was never going to end and then he licked me." "Licked you?" I said, confused. "You know?" she replied. "No, I don't know?" "He licked my pussy Zavia." "Noooooo", I said incredulously. "You're lying." "I swear on my life. He put his tongue on and in my pussy." "I'm in shock", I said. "Was it good?" "Yes. It was magnificent", she said as she fell back on my bed and smiled broadly at my ceiling. "Ok, that sounds pretty special in a way, I guess. I'm not really sure what to say next."

"Anyhow", she said. "Enough about me. What happened with you and Reece?". "We held hands and he asked to see me again some time," I said. "So when are you going to see him?" she asked. "I don't know. I think he was just being polite" "Hmmm, well I know he recently broke up with his girlfriend. So don't be so sure you won't hear from him. Anyhow, we've got a busy day planned so let's get moving. Go and take a shower then let's get some breakfast. Your mum is making pancakes and I want a share before they're all eaten."

I jumped out of bed. Pancakes was definitely an incentive. I grabbed my towel and headed to the bathroom in my parents' room as I knew it would be empty if my mum were in the kitchen. My dad was lying on the bed catching up on the week's newspapers. He raised his eyebrows as I walked in with my towel and said: "Can I help you Zavia?" "No Xavier. I'm fine thank you", I said cheekily. "I am just about to avail myself of your washroom facilities." He shook his head and said "you really do shit talk sometimes. Hurry up before your mother comes back and catches you in her bathroom and make sure you dry it down or else I'll get the blame". I ran over to him, gave him a hug and a kiss and said "Thanks, Daddy" before locking myself in my mum's beautiful bathroom that us kids weren't allowed to use. I had a quick shower and then bolted back past my dad into my room.

When I got back to my room, Zee was half laying on my bed fast asleep. I kicked her foot and said "You've got to be kidding me. Wake up Zee!" She jumped up and said "What? What? I was resting my eyes". "A likely story", I said as I pulled clothes out of my drawers trying to decide what to wear. I chose a short denim skirt with a vest and some boat shoes. "Quick Zee, let's get some breakfast." I said while pulling my door open and looking for signs of activity from the rest of the house. We raced down the stairs hoping that we were the first to reach the breakfast table and were pleasantly surprised to see that the only other person in the room, apart from my mum was my brother Lucky. Lucky's real name was Luke. He got the nickname Lucky because at 43 years old my mother didn't expect to get pregnant and based on all medical advice she thought it was unlikely that she would be able to carry to term. The doctors had also been concerned about the health implications for Luke if she did give birth to him. But despite all the concerns my mother carried him to term and he arrived strong and healthy. An additional reason was that he was born on my father's birthday, which we all took as a sign that he would be Lucky and there his nickname was born.

As Lucky was only a toddler, we didn't have much competition for the first batch of pancakes. Mum was expertly flipping them and talking on the phone. "Yes RaeRae I know that Rocco can be a handful but I'm sure he didn't mean to set the man's shoes on fire. Uh huh, yes I know." My mum said while rolling her eyes. I sniggered as it sounded like my cousin Rocco was in trouble again. Rocco was my mum's sister's son. Born a few months after me. Although he lived in London with my aunt Raechelle (aka RaeRae), he spent most Summers with us so that Aunty RaeRae could have a break. It meant that he, Adam, Zee and I were quite close as we were all around the same age. I loved having him around, he was the trickster of the group always playing tricks on people or making jokes. My mum made some excuse to Aunty RaeRae and clicked off, saying "I swear that boy will make my sister go grey before her time. Anyway Zavia, why haven't you given Zayasha something to drink? Where are your manners? That's no way to treat a guest".

Guest? I thought. Zee had been coming over to our house for breakfast since she was four years old and even had spare clothes here. So how was I supposed to consider her a guest? Zee was smiling. She loved to be fussed over by my mother. "Oh, thanks so much Aunty Gina. Zavia would it be an awful bother for me to have some freshly squeezed juice?" "Piss off" I mouthed at her while pouring her a glass of juice from the carton. I plonked it down on the table in front of her and curtsied with a giggle. Mum had finished the first stack of pancakes and placed them on the table between Zee and I. We both grabbed a pancake each and bit into them enthusiastically. "Pass the syrup Zee", I said through a mouthful of pancake. "Gosh, Zavia do you have to speak with your mouth full?" My mum reprimanded me shaking her head. "I tell you, sometimes I wonder whose child you are." I rolled my eyes and continued eating.

Once my mouth was empty, I said, "Oh yes mum, Zee has asked if I can go to her grandmother's birthday party this evening." "What time and where?" she said. "We'll pick Zavia up at about 7pm Aunty and it's at Everest Cricket Club." Said Zee. "Ok no problem, yes you can go and thank you Zayasha. What are you going to wear Zavia? I seem to remember that Lola bought you a short cocktail dress that would be perfect for this occasion". "Oh yeah, that would work, but I need shoes," I said. "How come you need shoes Zavia? What happened to the ones that Lola gave you with the dress?" "I burst the strap on them ages ago," I said. "Oh, Zavia! Why would you wait until now to tell me? Take some money from my purse and buy shoes to match it today when you go out. Zayasha said to me that you are going to town this morning". "Ok, thanks, Mum", I said smiling. Shopping was one of my favourite things to do.

Just as Zee and I got up from the table, Adam came ambling in, rubbing his eyes and yawning. "Ew, Adam. I can smell your armpits" I said. I usually said something derogatory to him instead of good morning. "Shut up Zavia. Hey Zee" he said "Hey Ads" she replied. Adam and Zee were quite close as well and on occasion hung out without me. I would have loved for them to be a couple but when I tried to set them up on a date they had told me in no uncertain terms that it would never happen. They were so emphatic I sometimes wondered if something had happened between them already which had put them off any further dating.

Zee and I excused ourselves from the kitchen and as it was still quite early, I put some plaits into Zee's hair before we left. She liked messy chic so wouldn't mind if there were some stray hairs later on in the evening. As I plaited her hair, I had to constantly remind her not to move. "Keep your head still please Zee", I said "or else this is going to take a very long time and we still have to go shopping and to the craft class." "Alright," she said impatiently. "That is a lot to get done today. We need a plan. What colour shoes do you want?" "Hmmm silver I think", I replied. "Ok, let's go to Candy's. They have an excellent selection of shoes and it's just next to where the craft class is." "Great," I said. "Let's leave at 10am". When the clock hit 10am, we jumped up, ready to start our busy day. Zee's hair was done and she managed to style it in such a way that it looked stylish instead of crazy.

As we got to the door, we saw Lola's car pulling up outside. I ran down to her and said "When did you get back? I thought you and Tyrone had left for Antigua". "Nah, Tyrone got a call to say that he needs to be in New York for a meeting next week so we cancelled our vacation." "Seems like he is always in New York these days. Do you think you guys will move there?" I asked her. "I don't know for sure, but it seems that way," she said. "Anyway, what are you and Zee doing today? I was just passing by to see if you wanted a lift into town. I'm going to get my hair done and I thought you would probably be going into town as well." I smiled and said "you know me so well. That's why you're my favourite sister". "Oh really? It's not because you look like me? We act like two peas in a pod and I spoil you then?" I laughed and said, "Well all of that too". When Lola said, we looked alike it was true. The only difference was that Lola had a more womanly figure. She had an ample bosom and wide hips. She hardly ever tied her hair so her curls hung free and she always dressed as if she was on her way out somewhere. Lots of dresses and heels or blazers and jeans. She had a unique and chic style. "A lift to Candy's would be great Lola", said Zee. Her skipping down the stairs interrupted my mental comparison of Lola and I. "Ok then, let me just talk to Ma for a couple of minutes and then I'll take you guys there before I go to my hair appointment." I was grateful for a lift because the public transport battle was too much on a Saturday morning when all the teenagers in Georgetown had the same idea as Zee and me.

The day went by in a flash. Luckily I was able to get the perfect shoes in Candy's leaving Zee and me with enough time to go to the craft class we had planned. Both of us were avid crafting fans. Zee liked to work with paints and draw and I was interested in jewellery and beading. We left the class with lots of new ways to do things and also some quirky pieces of jewellery. The next stop was my house, to get my clothes and drop off my jewellery. Zee and I decided it would be easier if we dressed together to help me avoid the endless bathroom queues at my house. Zee's house was completely different to mine. Although her father was a military man like my dad, Zee's house felt lived in and her parents were extremely laid back.

Zee and I were just putting the finishing touches on our hair and jewellery when her dad called up the stairs to us that we would be leaving in five minutes. Although we didn't expect to see anyone our own age, we still looked forward to our evening out and the opportunity to have a glass of wine each which was the limit set by our parents. One of the few approaches to parenthood that they all agreed on.

When we got to the party, we chose a table near the back of the room so that we could move in and out freely without everyone noticing.   As we sat watching people arrive and pick their seats we engaged in our favourite pastime of "people watching". We were amused to see Mr Beharry, one of Zee's grandmother's friends making a beeline to her as soon as he walked in. It was evident that he had a soft spot for her and Zee and I watched in amusement as he fussed over her while she acted impatient with him. He had clearly made a huge effort with his outfit and his shoes were well polished. He had a small gift bag in his hand and he strode purposefully over to her. I nudged Zee and said, "wow it's from Utopia Jewellery World, this should be interesting". Utopia was a high-end jeweller in the centre of town where you could get bespoke jewellery and gemstones. It would have cost serious bucks whatever it was. We leant forward to try to catch a glimpse of the actual size of the gift but we were too far away.

I was so busy focusing on poor Mr Beharry that I didn't even turn around when I heard the chair next to me being pulled out. It wasn't until I heard a cough next to me that I turned and found myself face to face with Reece. "Wow!" we both said simultaneously. "What are you doing here?" he said. "Mrs Wilson is Zee's grandma", I said. "Oh, small world", he replied. "She is one of my granny's best friends. So I'm here as her plus one. Would you believe this coincidence? I was honestly expecting to spend my whole evening making animals out of napkins to amuse myself". "Oooooh, can you do that?" I asked. "Show me, please. What animals can you do?" He looked at me and laughed. "No Zavia. I can't really do it. I was just saying that to emphasise how bored I would be". "Oh," I said feeling slightly silly. He touched my hand and said "you don't have to feel stupid about it. Your enthusiasm was kinda cute".

Zee had been watching us with interest but apparently she was also feeling a little bit left out so she interjected and said: "does anyone want another drink?" "Yes please", I said. "Another glass of wine would be good. Do you think we can get away with another glass each?" "Sure", she said, "I'll be back in a minute. Reece?" "No thanks", he said, "I'm driving, so it's best I stick to orange juice". "Ok", said Zee as she walked away. "So", said Reece turning back to me. "I enjoyed the game the other night and I wanted to invite you out again but I didn't have your number." "Yea I enjoyed it too", I said shyly. "Would tomorrow afternoon be too soon?" Reece asked. "I thought we could get some ice cream and go for a walk on the seawall." "That sounds great", I said. "I'll just need to ask my mum. Can I call you in the morning and let you know?" "Sure", he said as he smiled at me, his dimples becoming apparent. I hadn't even noticed them before nor had I noticed that sometimes his eyes looked grey like slate.

When Zee came back to the table, she had her cousin TJ with her. TJ was Zee's mum Kadeisha's nephew. He was a couple of years older than us and lived in Barbados. We didn't see him very often but I guess he had flown in for the party. "Hey TJ", I said. "Hey Zavia", he replied. Zee quickly introduced him to Reece and the four of us spent the evening cracking jokes, people watching and listening to the music played by the live band.

At the end of the night, Reece and I left a little early to walk out to the cars and say goodbye properly. As we walked through the grounds towards the car park, Reece took my hand. We walked for a few more steps when he stopped and looked at me. "Zavia, I hope that you can make it tomorrow." Then as he looked at me, he bent his head and kissed me. It was like a jolt of electricity coursing through my body. I felt like I was melting and I swear my knees buckled slightly. I leant into him and he pulled me closer. As I got lost in him and the kiss, a car horn blew and we jumped apart startled.

When we got to Zee's dad's car, TJ was playing music and lounging in the driver's seat. "How did you get here so quickly?" I said. "I thought that we left you in the hall." "I went round the other way", he said. "Zee walks too slowly and I was ready to jet. I'm gonna stay at Aunty Kadeisha's house tonight so Uncle Zeph said I can spin you and Zee home and then come back for him and Aunty." "Ok cool," I said. "Is Zayasha's dad actually called Zeph?" Reece whispered to me. "No," I said. "His name is Zephaniah but everyone calls his Zeph for short" "Oh ok," said Reece, still sounding confused. We stood side by side listening to the music TJ was playing until Zee came strolling up to the car. "Ready?" I said pointedly "It's not like we've been waiting or anything" she laughed and said, "I was trying to get one of the waiters' numbers". I shook my head and muttered, "what happened to Gerald?" "Pardon?" Said Reece. "Nothing", I said hurriedly. "Well I guess this is goodbye until tomorrow", Reece said giving me a hug goodbye. "Bye", I said as I climbed into the back of the car. As TJ pulled out of the parking lot, I waved goodbye to Reece and stared at him until he was just a speck in the distance. "You really like him don't you?" said Zee. "Yes I think I do", I said smiling. TJ rolled his eyes and said, "you girls are so pathetic". Zee playfully punched his arm and said "shut up. I bet you have a girlfriend you go mad over back in BIM". He shook his head and said "I don't go crazy over no gyal" and we all laughed. As we pulled up in front of my house, I saw the curtains twitching in my parent's room. "I see Aunty Gina is still up Zav", Zee said laughing. "Yep", I said, "just my luck!"

As I fumbled for my keys in my bag, my mother opened the door and said: "who was that driving Zeph's car?" "It was TJ, Mum. Aunty Kadeisha's nephew from Barbados". "Oh yes", my mum said, "Kacey's son. How is Kacey?" "I didn't see her. I don't think she came for this trip," I said. "How come you're still awake?" I asked. "Lucky had a nightmare and woke me up," she said, "Then I couldn't go back to sleep and as your father isn't home yet either, I stayed up watching television". "Oh, what are you watching?" I said following her up the stairs. "Just an old episode of Golden Girls. I needed a laugh", she said. I wandered into her room and sat on the edge of her bed to take my shoes off. I laughed when I saw my baby brother Lucky snuggled up under the covers. I guessed now was a good a time as any to ask to go out with Reece the next day. "Mum, I saw Reece at the party. He was there with his grandma." "Reece?" she said quizzically. "Oh yes, Reece Rodrigues. That was sweet of him to accompany his granny." "Yes it was", I said, "anyway," I continued rushing my words. "He wants to take me out for ice cream on the seawall tomorrow. Is that ok? I'll be home by 7pm." "Do you have homework?" "Yes", I said, "I did, but it's all done already". "And you'll be home by 7pm on the dot?" "Yes", I said. "Well, that's fine. You're 16 now so you need to start making your own choices, within reason, so I'm happy for you to go. "But", she said, "I want to meet him. So make sure he picks you up from here". "Ok mum", I said jumping up and giving her a kiss on the cheek. She laughed and shooed me away. "Be quiet", she said, "or you'll wake Lucky and then I promise, I'm going to make you stay up with him". I smiled and said, "that isn't a problem you know I love Lucky". "I know", she said smiling. "You spoil him as much as Lola spoils you. Pull my door in all the way", she told me as I left her room.

That night I slept fitfully waking up every minute with excitement. I couldn't believe I would be going on a date with Reece the next day. As the sun cracked through my curtains, I got up and stretched. I couldn't believe it was morning already. I looked at the time and saw it was 8am. On a Sunday, I could stay in bed until at least

9am before most of the family stirred. I lay there thinking about what I would wear and what colour to paint my nails. In a way, this was my first proper date and I was looking forward to it so much. I couldn't wait to tell Zee and, of course, to call Reece to confirm. Just as I dozed back off, I heard my door being pushed open and a little voice whispered: "ZavZav are you awake?" I turned to see my baby brother standing in my doorway. I smiled and said, "I'm not really awake but you can come and lie down with me". "Can I watch cartoons?" he said. I nodded and he ran into my room and jumped into my bed as I turned my TV on. I loved his smell and at 14 years my junior he could technically have been my own child. I loved him more than any of my other siblings. We lay next to each other watching cartoons with Lucky giggling and me trying to savour the last few minutes of peace.

At almost 9am on the dot, I heard Adam's bedroom door open and he stomped to the bathroom making enough noise to wake the whole house. I rolled my eyes and thought *here we go*. My mother's footsteps were the next ones that I heard walking down the hallway. I could smell her perfume so knew that she was already showered and ready for the day. She knocked on my door while calling out "Lucky, you need to come and prepare for church". He snuggled in deeper and I covered him with my sheet as if that would hide him from our mother. She came into my room and stood next to the bed looking at my sheets all bundled up and smiled saying "Zav, have you seen Lucky?" "No Mum", I replied and he hugged me tighter, giggling under the covers. The three of us played this little game most Sunday mornings and I was always filled with so much love for this little boy.

Lucky was fidgeting and Mum grabbed him kicking and screaming. His little face was all crumpled and I felt sorry for him so I told my mother that I would get him ready and give her one less thing to do. "Thanks, Zav", she said, "I'll go down and get breakfast started". I pushed the covers off us and took Lucky from Mum. Then I walked into the hallway with him in my arms and peeked into my parents' room. My mother had laid out a pale blue dress to wear so I decided to take out a matching outfit for Lucky. I went into the room he shared with JoJo and took out a pair of navy blue shorts with a light blue waistcoat and a white shirt. I knew he would look adorable. As I was already there, I chose JoJo's outfit as well so she would match Mum and Lucky.

At eight years old JoJo liked to look pretty and a bit older than she was so I chose a flared blue skirt with a floral blouse and white cardigan. I was feeling rather pleased with my choices and smiled as I imagined how cute they would look together. I showered Lucky and sent him down to get some breakfast before I dressed him so he wouldn't mess up his clothes. Then my mother sent JoJo up to me to get her hair done. Being the eldest girl currently living at home, I had to help with my younger siblings. I found it annoying mostly but sometimes I didn't mind too much, especially when they weren't naughty.

Once, Mum, JoJo and Lucky had left for church, the house was quiet. Adam and I didn't have to go to church every week so we were at home with our father following our non-church Sunday morning ritual. I looked forward to these breakfasts with my father, reading newspapers and debating current affairs. It was a special time for all of us. A rite of passage that I had enviously watched my older siblings enjoy while waiting to grow old enough to share this experience.

As Dad cooked our breakfast that included bakes (or fried dumplings) and salt fish and eggs, I called Reece. I took the cordless telephone into my bedroom and dialled his number nervously. "Hello Rodrigues residence", a female voice said. "Hello. May I speak to Reece, please?" "I'm sorry Reece is at church. Can I take a message?" "Yes. Could you please ask him to call Zavia on 56327?" "I will", she said and the phone clicked off. I took the phone back downstairs feeling a bit deflated but as soon as I smelt the hot bakes, I cheered up again. Dad had laid the newspapers out on the table and Adam was already looking at the headlines. I took my seat inhaling the breakfast smells before reaching for a paper. Today's headline was all about a cyanide spill caused by the massive mining company, Amaya Ltd. Some streams and rivers had been contaminated and people who had been using water from them were ill. Dad came in and laid the last dish on the table and said: "Adam can you go to the pantry and bring up some juice before we start to eat please?" "Sure Dad", Adam said and ran down to the pantry, which was in the basement.

"Right", Dad said, "today's question is whether or not the government should prohibit Amaya Ltd from continuing operations in Guyana". "Get them out", Adam said immediately and emphatically. My father smiled and said "let's eat first and then start the debate. Remember you have to justify your point of view". "Ok", said Adam while helping himself to a generous serving of fish and about eight bakes. "Wow, Adam. Hungry are you?" I said sarcastically. "Yea I'm a growing boy Zav", he said and I laughed.

"So how has your week been, both of you?" Dad said. He wasn't home very much so this was his chance to catch up with us and I really loved that he let very little interfere with our fortnightly Sunday morning routine. "Well, we've been working on our university applications," said Adam. "I'm wavering between staying here and going to the University of Guyana or studying in London or even Jamaica with the twins." We had an older twin brother and sister, Aidan and Audrey, who were 20. They lived and studied in Jamaica.

"What subjects have you narrowed it down to this week?" said my father. It was a standing joke that for the last three months Adam's choices had changed almost as frequently as his underwear. "Well, I'm quite sure that I want to run a business here when I get older. So I'm thinking about something in the hospitality industry or business management. "Hmm", said my father. "Hospitality is a soft subject that only girls would study and even then only the girls who have absolutely no chance of passing any other exam. Frankly I won't be paying for you to study hospitality. Business Management sounds more reasonable but also strikes me as lacking sustainability and transferability. Have you considered Accountancy? You're a natural mathematician and you passed your Principle of Accounts exam with flying colours. I think you should consider it." "Ok, Dad", he said. "Let me think about it.

"What about you Zavia?" "Because Adam and I were so close in age we started school at the same time so were at the same educational level. "Well, before I tell you what I want to do. I'd like to refute your sexist view about hospitality. If it's a useless qualification then it is equally useless for both men and women. Not just men thank you very much." My father smiled and said, "in all fairness that is pretty much what I said except I referenced women specifically, which was sexist, so I apologise". "Thank you", I said graciously. "Anyway. My choice is Human Resource Management. I'm interested in what people do and why and I'm also good at people watching and observing which are useful skills in HR." "Hmmm", my father said. "I'm not sure, but you have said it's what you wanted to do for the last three months so I will support you if you still choose it at graduation time. Where do you want to study?" he said. "I'd like to study in America" I replied. "Ok. Well get your applications ready and let's see what happens when all your exam results are in. You have four months left so keep focused. When will we get your predicted grades?" "At the end of this month", I said and Adam winced.

"I saw that Adam", my father said sternly. "Is there anything you'd like to tell me before your grades come in?" "No sir", Adam replied hesitantly. "I only ask because you seem to be skirt-chasing more than studying and specifically I was told that you and Brigadier Johnson's daughter have gotten close in recent weeks." Adam actually blushed a little and said "No sir, I'm still focused on my studies." My father broke into a smile and said "it's ok to chase girls too you know. I was a bit of a skirt chaser in my day. It's how I ended up getting your mother pregnant when she was sixteen. We used to......" "Whoa, whoa, whoa, Dad. We really don't need to hear any more about you and Mum dating thanks." Adam and I protested loudly. My father shook his head and said "we didn't have nine children through immaculate conception you know". I grimaced and said "Ok, ok. We get it. You and Mum had sex. Feel better now?" "Had", he said, "why are you using the past tense? There's still life in the old dog yet. How do you think Lucky came along?"

"Ok!" I said. "Time to start the debate I think. Let's clear the table and then we can get started". Adam stacked all the dishes up and took them into the kitchen. We would wash up together afterwards. As I was piling the dishes in the sink, the telephone rang. I answered the kitchen phone and heard a silky smooth voice saying "Hello. May I speak to Zavia, please?" "Hi", I said, "this is Zavia". "Hey Zavia, it's Reece. I heard you called me earlier?" "Yes, yes I did," I said. "I wanted to confirm that I can come out today. I need to be back home by 7pm and my mum wants to meet you. Can you meet me at my house?" "Ok", he said, "that's great. I'll pick you up at 3.30pm. I'll park my car at your house then we can walk?" "Perfect," I said, "sorry I can't talk but it's our Sunday debate so we'll catch up when I see you". "Sunday debate?" he asked. "I'll explain when I see you later" I responded. We disconnected the call and I smiled, excited by the prospect of seeing him later that day.

As I walked back to the dining room, I mentally prepared for the debate. I knew what my stance was but wanted Adam to go first. Adam's opening gambit was to repeat "get rid of them all!" I chuckled as my father asked him to justify his position. He ranted about it being the right thing to do and the fact that the natural habitat in Guyana is more important than building the wealth of a foreign and privately owned company. Once he had set out his position my father turned to me. My position was that the company should be told to rectify the damage caused and make new provisions to ensure that there wasn't a recurrence. I also suggested that the Government take this opportunity to renegotiate the contracts ensuring that environmental considerations were built into the process.

Dad nodded and said," Adam, what did you think of Zavia's proposal?" Adam sighed and said "well I guess it would be easier to sell to the company but I do question whether or not they would take any notice. These things need a hard line". "Zavia, how do you respond?" "I do think that people might ignore the clauses but a hard-line approach makes this war before it needs to be in my opinion". My father nodded and said "I think both of you have made valid points but in this case, Zavia has shown more strategic thinking. Adam, you're sometimes too fast to put forward what you want without thinking of how you can negotiate. Together, though, you would make a formidable team." We both smiled at Dad's way of always ending the debates by reminding us to be united instead of competitive. "Right! Now washing up time", he said. Adam and I spent the next hour washing up and listening to music in the kitchen. Once we had cleaned the kitchen, we were free to do whatever we wanted with the rest of our day.

I spent the rest of my day studying and waiting for when I would be going out with Reece. At 3.30pm promptly the doorbell rang and I bounded down the stairs. My mother had already opened the door and was ushering Reece into the house. "Pleased to meet you, Mrs Fraser. You have a beautiful home", he said. My mother beamed while I rolled my eyes and thought I need this to end quickly before Dad or Adam turn up. "Hi Reece", I said. "This is my mum. She went to school with your dad and aunts." "Cool", he said. "I'll tell Dad that I met you." "Right", I said, "let's go". "Do you want a drink?" My mum asked him trying to prolong the conversation. Before he could answer, I replied "no we'll get something when we're out" and dragged him outside. "Phew!" I said. "Thankfully we got out of there before she launched into the full-scale investigative mode. My mother's very inquisitive. She probably would've had your shoe size, shirt size and a list of all your hopes and dreams before we left." Reece chuckled and said "she can't be that bad" and I looked at him in mock anguish. "No, she isn't really", I said, "after all she made a beautiful specimen like me". He

41

laughed and said, "your modesty knows no limits!"

As we walked towards the Seawall, we talked about his studies at university. He was planning to be a journalist and I was interested in his views on politics. I was especially impressed when he started talking about the current situation with Amaya Ltd. "Oh that was what our debate was about this morning", I said. "Oh yeah. Your debate" he said, "what was that all about?" "Well," I said, "my dad introduced the Sunday Debate years ago for my siblings when they became teenagers. He thinks that it helps us to articulate our views and prepare for our adulthood as reasoned, reflective activists. I secretly think he wants one of us to catch the political bug by doing it but he's still waiting". "That's really cool", Reece said. "Your dad sounds like an amazing man. Kinda different from the norm". "Yea he's quite cool", I said 'but quite strict as well". "So what was your view of the situation?" he asked. I explained my opinion and Reece listened intently. "Wow, Zavia you're a very smart girl. I think that you could go into politics if you wanted to. Is it something that you think you would get into?" "Erm, I never really thought about it", I said. "I just know I want to do something enterprising and politics never really seemed to fit the bill." "You look like a natural politician to me", he said. "You're passionate, animated and your arguments are convincing. You should think about it". I blushed, unaccustomed to being complimented by a young man on something other than my physical attributes.

We walked in companionable silence until we got to the Seawall. The Seawall is exactly as it sounds. It's a wall that creates a barrier between the sea and the land. The sea is actually the Atlantic Ocean so technically it is the Ocean Wall but the name Seawall seems to have stuck. Reece had a rucksack and as we walked along the wall, we looked out across the horizon in silence. The majesty of the ocean always left me awestruck and today was no different. As we walked, I felt Reece slip his hand into mine and it felt good and right walking with him a hand in hand. We were approaching the Umana Yana and the Pegasus Hotel so we stepped down and sat on one of the many benches dotted along the approach. Reece put down his rucksack and pulled out a bottle of drink for each of us and some snacks. "Well aren't you just Mr Prepared?" I said laughing. "Yea, I thought it would be fun to have a little mini picnic together."

As we talked, it became evident that we had a lot in common. Reece told me about his ex-girlfriend being more interested in partying and seeking the attention of lots of guys rather than just being content with him. He explained that though he went out sometimes he was still content to just go to the Seawall and relax but she was much more party and alcohol oriented. I nodded and explained that I seemed to meet guys intent on deflowering me as part of an overall plan to collect virgins as trophies. I explained to him that he was the first person I had just talked to and it was refreshing. He smiled and said, "most of my friends would think that I'm a pussy for not trying to get straight into your panties". I smiled and said, "don't you want to get into my panties?" "I'm going to choose not to answer that", he said blushing. I laughed flirtatiously. He was so cute and kind that it was possible that I would be begging to get into his pants, not the other way around.

Suddenly I heard the sound of a snow cone cart. "I love snow cones", I said, "I'm gonna get us some." As I went to get up, he grabbed my hand and said "No, I'll get them. I don't let women pay for things." I looked at him thinking that he was kind of old fashioned but it felt nice. I watched him go over to the snow cone man. He came back with our cones dripping with condensed milk. I licked at it enthusiastically savouring the taste. "I haven't had one of these for ages," I said as I expertly licked the milk in circles. "Ahem, Zavia. Though I'm not going to jump you, I have to say that the way you are licking that snow cone is distracting me." I blushed again and said "Oh, I wasn't trying to distract you. I was just enjoying my snow cone." "I'm sorry", he said, "I didn't mean to make you uncomfortable. It was a joke." "It's ok", I said "but do guys really like that? I mean to be licked and slobbered on? It doesn't sound very sexy to me". "Ok, this is taking a weird turn", he said. "Honestly, only one person has ever done it to me, but yea it's kinda nice. It isn't as disgusting as it sounds and it feels good." "Yuck", I said and he laughed. "There's that innocent side of yours again." I smiled slightly disappointed at the way the conversation was going and sure that he wouldn't want to see me again.

Reece was a great catch but now it looked like this would be our first and last proper date because of my immaturity. A shiver ran down my spine not just because I felt a little sad but also because a brisk breeze had just blown in from across the ocean. Reece leant down and rummaged through his bag pulling out a sweatshirt. He threw it over my shoulders and I jumped as I felt his arms around me. "What? Don't you want me to touch you?" He said. "It's not that" I replied "I just…. you know. I wanted to impress you but instead, I've

43

come across as some snivelling little girl." "No, that's not how you've come across at all", he said. He turned my face towards his and said "you aren't a snivelling little girl. You're amazing. You're beautiful and you're funny. You interest me and I feel like I could listen to you all day". I looked up at him in surprise and he kissed me lightly on the lips. I felt so happy at that moment like I'd never felt before. We broke the kiss and then sat there with me huddled in his arms. I felt him stretch his arm out and he groaned. "It's almost quarter to seven Zavi. It's time to get you home." "Zavi?" I said. "I like that. No one calls me Zavi". He smiled and said "I'm not just anybody". As we walked towards my house, I remember wondering if this was what love was supposed to feel like.

For the next nine months, Reece and I were inseparable. My mother liked him and my father hadn't said anything bad about him which was a minor miracle. He was respectful and quiet and he never pressured me into sex although he did have a very clear idea of how our relationship would be conducted. We petted heavily and I learnt a few tricks which made my snow cone skills pale in comparison, but we didn't have full intercourse and I felt comfortable with that.

Because my parents liked Reece they were quite lenient about our relationship. He would often stay at our house until quite late and even occasionally stayed the night although he was only allowed to sleep in Adam's room or on the sofa. I was also invited to stay at his house but my parents, especially my father, would never allow it.

On my 17th birthday, Reece planned a day of surprises for me. I half expected part of the surprise to be a night in a hotel where we could consummate our relationship because we had been together for nine months but I couldn't have been more wrong. Straight after breakfast with my family, Reece arrived to collect me. I was intrigued and the broad smile on my mother's face made me more suspicious. I settled into the passenger seat and Reece told me to get comfortable as we were going for a long drive. We zipped up the highway along the East Bank of the Demerara River and I wondered what we would possibly be doing there. As we passed the turn for Timerhi, where the airport, was, I said to Reece "why are we going up to Linden?" "I have something I want to show you", he replied.

After about an hour, we arrived in the town and I was surprised at the way he expertly navigated the streets which were all completely unfamiliar to me. "How come you know your way around so well?" I said. "It makes sense that I would know my way around my future home doesn't it?" "Future home?" I said quizzically. "Aaah Zavia be patient. All will be revealed." As we passed the centre of town and approached the outskirts, we saw some vacant fenced plots of land shaped into what seemed to be new streets. At the end of one of these emerging streets, Reece pulled onto a bridge in front of a vacant lot and turned the car off. "Why are we here?" I said surveying the location. It was full of trees and bushes that still needed to be cleared including a laden mango tree. "At least whoever buys this lot won't ever run out of mangoes", I said and Reece laughed. "The things that you think of sometimes amaze me Zavia." "Well it's true," I said. "I'd make pickle and sour and mango drink every day if that tree were mine." "Be careful what you wish for?" he said as he unchained the gate and pushed it open beckoning me to step inside. "What do you mean? I'm getting sick of all the riddles", I said. "Ok, calm down. This was a birthday gift from my grandma for my 18th birthday last year. For my 20th birthday in two months, my parents are going to start building my house for me." "Wow", I said. "How the other half live." He smiled and said, "it's not my fault that my family is rich." "I know", I said, "I didn't mean to sound like that. It's good that they can help you." "Well", he said. "To be honest, they're helping us because I have a question for you", and as I looked at him he dropped to one knee and pulled a small red box out of his pocket. I frowned and said, "what are you doing?" "Zavia", he said. "I want to know whether you would do me the honour of becoming my wife?" I looked at him speechless unable to answer as he slipped the ring onto my finger. It was a beautiful solitaire diamond set in a rich rose-toned gold ring. I smiled because he had remembered that my favourite colour was pink.

"Aren't we too young to get married?" I asked. "Well, I'll be 21 before we get married and you'll be 18. I don't want to wait too long because I may be forced to have sex with you before we're married and that wouldn't be right." "But you've given me a ring now." I said, "it wouldn't really be a sin would it?" "Yes", he said. "It would and I firmly believe that sex before marriage is wrong. I want you to be my first, as my wife and I'm sure about that". "Ok," I said, still feeling a little unsure. I wasn't desperate to have sex but recently when we were kissing, I felt a deeper stirring in the pit of my stomach. I was getting curious about how it would feel to be made love to. I stared at the ring sparkling on my finger lost in my thoughts. I was jolted out of my reverie by Reece's voice saying "there's more to your surprise than this my dear". As he stood there beaming from ear to ear looking really proud of himself, I felt a momentary flash of annoyance. He hadn't even waited for me to officially accept his proposal. He had assumed that my answer was yes. But as quickly as it came to my annoyance passed.

He led me back to the car and as I climbed in I wondered what more he could surprise me with. I also wondered what on earth my parents would make of this latest development. I was always the child who pushed the boundaries and did as I liked but this seemed like a step too far, even for me. As we drove through the unfamiliar streets of Linden, I sat back and basked in the sunlight coming through the window. Reece turned into the town centre and I found myself looking up and down Linden's version of Main Street with all the shops I was used to seeing in Georgetown. We stopped in front a restaurant called Rita's and I smiled thinking of my granny who had the same name. As I went to get out, he told me to wait and ran around to open my door. I rolled my eyes feeling another flash of annoyance at his eager puppy act. I was getting fed up already which wasn't a good sign considering it seemed as if I had just agreed to marry him.

As we walked into Rita's, the waiter looked meaningfully at Reece as he gave his name and told us to go up the stairs. Walking up the stairs, I heard the sound of other diners. It sounded really busy. As we got to the top of the stairs, I heard a range of voices shout "SURPRISE!" Some sounded familiar and as I scanned the room, I saw my family, friends and Reece's family standing together clapping and smiling under a banner that said *Happy Birthday and Congratulations*. I felt like I had been hit by a tonne of bricks and my breath caught in my throat at the enormity of the situation. I felt like I was suffocating and I couldn't seem to stop the feeling of the walls closing in on me. Reece was willing me to move further into the room and I stiffly let him guide me while fixing a smile on my face.

My mother came gliding over, enjoying the moment as the queen of this expensive and decadent show. She gave me a hug and said "I'm really happy for you baby. This will be a marriage made in heaven. You're lucky to be welcomed into such an auspicious family. The world will be your oyster and oh my grandbabies will be the most adorable little things". I looked at her incredulously and said "Mum how much have you had to drink? It's only 2pm". She sniggered and said "whatever Zavia, whatever!" I looked around and said, "where's Daddy?" "He's on the terrace smoking", she replied. I frowned, Dad smoking was hardly ever a good sign so I excused myself and went to find him. It took me awhile to get to the terrace door as I kept getting accosted by guests wanting to congratulate me and ogle the ring.

Finally, I got to the terrace and found my dad smoking cigars with his brother, Uncle Compton. They were both swirling ice in identical tumblers of brandy with identical gold rings gracing their fingers. I watched them thinking that these two men were truly my favourite two men in the world. As I walked over to them, Uncle Compton looked up and hummed the Bridal March. My father grimaced and swigged from his glass before turning to me and smiling, but his smile didn't reach his eyes. "What's wrong Daddy?" I said as I slipped my arm around his waist and snuggled under his armpit. "Nothing baby" he replied. "No", I said forcefully "something IS wrong and I want to know what it is". "Nothing," he said equally forcefully. "You want to get married and I'll support you. I may not understand your decision, especially because you have all the tools to be a strong independent woman. You didn't need to marry for position and status. You would have earned that all for yourself." "What do you mean I want to get married Daddy? I'm as surprised as you are by this turn of events." My father's eyes narrowed and Uncle Compton's eyebrows raised slightly. "What do you mean you're surprised by it all?" he asked. "I thought it was just about my birthday today," I said. "But then Reece proposed to me at the vacant lot his grandmother bought him and before I knew it the ring was on my finger and we were here celebrating." "Zavia, tell me something. Do you want to get married?" My father asked. "I don't know. I've never thought about it." "Well, child you need to think about it sooner rather than later because things are moving quickly." "You're not pregnant are you?" Uncle Compton asked as my father cut his eyes on him. I rolled my eyes and said "No Uncle, I'm not pregnant. I've never even had sex with him." My father looked uncomfortable and said, "as usual you forget I'm your father, Zavia". "Oh, really Daddy. Don't you remember the Sunday debate when you were talking about sex?" Uncle Compton laughed and said, "You sure dis boy ain't gay?" "Yes Uncle", I said, "I'm sure he isn't gay." My father set down his glass, covered his ears and said: "Can we talk about something else please?" I giggled and squeezed his waist always struck by how such a small man could command such great respect and attention.

"But on a serious note baby." My father said while turning my chin so that I was looking at him. "You need to decide what you're going to do. Marriage is a big commitment. You need to be sure that you are compatible in every way." We heard the terrace door open and Reece strode over "oh there you are Zavi. My mum wants to get a picture with us". "Her name is Zavia, asswipe!" I heard Uncle Compton mutter. I threw him a dirty look and prayed that Reece hadn't heard him. I looked at my father who was sniggering like a schoolboy and sipping his brandy. My uncle and father had given me a lot to think about.

As Reece and I re-entered the restaurant, we were met by his mother and an older man. "This is my grandfather", said Reece. "He lives in England, but he came over for the engagement party." I looked at Reece and said, "how long have you been planning this?" "About a month", he replied. "I knew you were the one for me. Grandpa wanted to meet you now because he's a pastor and he'll be marrying us. It's a family tradition." My head was spinning as Reece's grandfather embraced me warmly. Although I knew that I wanted to get married at some point, I hadn't thought that it would be so early. At the same time, though, I knew that Reece would be successful and wealthy in his own right. He was a modern Prince Charming and most girls would give their right arm to be in my position.

As I was thinking, Zee came over and pulled me to the bathroom. Once we knew that the bathroom was empty, she turned to me and said "have you seen what Reece's cousin Portia is wearing? Considering this is a daytime event, she looks more like she's going to the Oscars or something. Idiot!" "You're too much you know Zee" I replied. "Also", she added, "you kept this whole engagement thing quiet. How come you didn't tell me that you were going to get engaged?" "Because I didn't know", I said. "I didn't have a clue until he proposed". "Shut up!" she replied incredulously. "Who does that? How do you feel about it? Can't say that I thought you would be married off so quickly. Are you pregnant?" I shook my head and said "No Zee. That's impossible. Also, you would have been the first person I told if I were." "Yea good point", she said, "so what's the rush?" "He's a committed virgin", I said, "he wants to get married so that we can start the rest of our life". "Wow that's a desperate move to get pussy", she said. I punched her arm and said, "you're so stupid Zee. Seriously, I have to make up my mind because it's all moving so quickly". "That's kinda an understatement!" She said and I rolled my eyes. "Anyhow let's go and enjoy the party. The food is fantastic and the booze is free" "Cheers to that", Zee replied and we linked our arms and went back to the party.

As dusk approached Reece explained that we would be staying over in Linden until the morning and then we would drive back. "Are my parents staying too?" I asked and he said, "No we're staying to go to my cousin's birthday party." The party was fun. Reece's cousin James had spared no expense. The DJ was talented and created a good vibe and Reece was great company. It made me think that being married to him might be fun and as we danced to the last song of the night swaying together, I imagined how we would be on our wedding day. I smiled and squeezed him hard and said: "I can't wait to be your wife".

A month later I was preparing for my university placement. As part of the coursework grades for my business studies exam, I had to attend a four-week Enterprise course at the University of Guyana (UG). On the day of enrolment, students from across the country came together to get their group assignments. Each group had four people. I was the team leader. My teammates were Nicholas Roberts, Jake Jackson and Anna Williams. I didn't recognise any of their names.

As I walked into our assigned meeting room, I was glad it was empty so that I could take the seat facing the door and watch as people arrived. First, a wild-haired girl walked in whom I assumed was Anna. "Hi, I'm Zavia", I said offering my hand. "Great to meet you, I'm Anna", she said ignoring my hand and leaning to hug me. As she let go, a serious looking boy walked in. He had short brown hair and piercing blue eyes and said his name was Jake and he was studying accountancy and economics. Anna's response was "Oh! Are we pitching for roles? Well, I'm your communications, marketing, sales and PR person. I love talking to people and understanding what they need. I love your glasses, Jake. Your eyes are really piercing. With those blue eyes, you should probably wear more water like tones rather than the earthy browns and beiges you appear to favour." Jake looked at her like she was from another planet and said: "When does this meeting start?" "We're just waiting for Nicholas", I said. The door creaked opened and a medium build guy with a basketball under his arm strolled in. I mentally rolled my eyes thinking that as an athlete he probably didn't have the same intellectual capacity as me. I hoped that Anna, Jake and I wouldn't have to bear the brunt of the work to make up for his likely academic shortcomings.

"Right. Now Nicholas is here, let's get started." As I spoke, Nicholas moved to stand at the flip chart and said: "so what ideas have we all got for businesses?" I was a little annoyed and said: "I think it's my job to lead the discussion". "Ok Boss", he said "whatever you want Boss" and threw the flip chart pen at me. I caught it and said "thanks" while feeling pissed off at his obviously patronising tone. "Ok", I said, "Anna, as you're the creative one do you want to start?" "Sure", she said, as she got up and skipped to the flip chart enthusiastically. "Can each of you tell me what you want to do? Jake, you first." "I don't know what I want to do", he said, "but I don't want to sell products. I think I prefer selling services". "Hmmm interesting", Anna said, "I love that you didn't answer that in the way I expected. Edgy! I like it!" Jake looked at her like she was crazy again and I can't say I blamed him. She was like no one I had ever met before. It was very disconcerting. "What about you Nicholas?" she said. "Well I wanted to try promotions and events management" he replied, "And you Zavia?" "My idea was events management too", I said. "Awesome," she said. "My idea was a Marketing and PR company." "Ok", I said, an idea formulating in my mind. "What do you guys think about us planning events and then marketing and resourcing them ourselves? That would fit everyone's criteria." "Hmmm", Jake, Anna and Nicholas said in unison. "Sounds like I good idea", Nicholas said grudgingly. "Yea I like it" agreed Jake and Anna sighed and said "wow! We are in perfect alignment". I looked at her checking to see whether or not she was kidding, but her face was totally serious. Thankfully it was only four weeks that I would have to work with her so I probably wouldn't kill her before the end of the placement.

"Great, so let's think of a name for the business", I said. We all sat there silently pondering; Jake was chewing the top of his pen while Anna was sitting with her eyes closed humming softly and rocking. *I swear this bitch is on some kinda drugs* I thought chuckling inwardly. Nicholas got up and starting sketching on the flipchart. I watched him with interest. I was drawing a blank and waiting for the big reveal from him was more interesting. As he stepped away from the flipchart, I smiled at what he had sketched

JAzZiN

It was perfect and so obvious, a mixture of our initials. I laughed spontaneously and said "sometimes simple really is better. Now let's split the team in half with one pair focusing on planning and the other on sponsorship". "I want to work with Jake", said Anna "We seem like a good fit." Jake looked at me imploringly but frankly Anna made a valid point. Her creativity combined with his flair for numbers would make them a good team and I knew I didn't want to work with her. "That leaves me and you Nicholas", I said and he replied, "yeah looks like it".

Nicholas pulled his chair next to mine and said: "shall we start writing the business plan?" "Cool," I said. As we worked, I was struck by the fact that Nicholas was far from being a mindless athlete. He had a sharp mind and we worked well together. We developed a plan to host a Fashion Show, which we shared with Anna and Jake. "This is all sounding fantastic", said Anna once we had explained it to them. "My dad runs Jupiter Press so I can get posters designed and printed and we can use one of my dad's meeting rooms at Jupiter as a base as well, if you want?" "That's great Anna", said Jake. "I'll set up base there as our Operations Director." I smiled as the plan seemed to be coming together.

By 5pm, I felt mentally exhausted but excited about the project. "Do you wanna grab something to eat at the cafeteria?" said Nicholas to me. "I'm not sure?" I said, "it depends on if my ride is here or not". "Cool", he said, as Anna and Jake said, "yeah, we're gonna go to the cafeteria, we're starving". As we packed up, I watched Nicholas tear down the flip chart page and hand it over to Anna so that she could recreate the logo on our posters and promotional materials. He was meticulous and considered, which seemed at odds with the basketball under his arm. "Do you actually play basketball?" I enquired. Nicholas looked at me and smiled and said "nope" "so what's with the ball?" I said. He laughed and replied, "that would be telling".

As we walked out of the room, I could hear shouts from the basketball court indicating that a game was in progress. We walked towards the court on our way to the cafeteria. Nicholas was bouncing the ball and his dribbling skills seemed quite well developed for someone who claimed not to play basketball. When we turned the corner, we saw that a fast-paced game was in progress. We wandered over to the sidelines. I noticed Reece's car parked in a space near the court and scanned the crowd looking for him before I saw him on the court. *Great!* I thought now I'd have to wait even longer to eat as he would expect me to watch him. He was playing on a team with some of his friends and the other team appeared to be led by Craig one of the guys who used to go to my school.

As we looked for seats, I noticed Craig signal for a time out and he looked towards us. I wondered what had happened and felt even more confused when Craig came bounding towards us "Hey Nicky" he said, "You wanna bounce?" "Sure", said Nicholas. "Yo Mike, get off the court. Nicky's gonna take your spot" Craig shouted. "Aw man", said the guy who I assumed was Mike, "no complaints," said Craig "we need Nicky's skills. We're 10 points down". "Ok", said Mike sullenly. Nicholas stretched and shrugged off his t-shirt and ran to join the game. As I watched the game, I was shocked by the skills that Nicholas had. He was fast and accurate and I noticed that his ability was annoying the hell out of Reece. It annoyed him so much that five minutes before the end of the game, as Nicholas tried to drive a three-pointer home to win, Reece ran at him and pushed him to the ground. The referee whistled to signal the foul but by now Nicholas and Reece were rolling around the court throwing punches at each other. I was taken aback. I knew that Reece was sometimes competitive, but he wasn't usually this aggressive. Then again, he was usually the dominant force on the court so I guessed that Nicky's prowess had ignited some kind of insecurity in him. As all the guys swarmed around trying to pull them apart, I observed them feeling disgusted. When the fight was finally stopped the referee awarded Nicholas a free throw and Reece was sent off the court. Reece walked over to me looking sullen and I shook my head at him. "Let's go", he said. "No, I wanna finish watching the game. It's just five more minutes", I said. Reece grumbled and bent to tie his laces while I watched Nicholas take the free throw. Nicholas regained possession of the ball and scored another three-pointer. He was a fantastic player and I found myself cheering and clapping as the final whistle blew. Reece looked at me sour faced and said: "We lost Zavia, you aren't supposed to be cheering". "Well it was an exciting game", I said and "I'm not that bothered about who won. "Yea whatever," he said, "Are you ready for me to take you home?" "Yes I'm ready", I said, "but aren't we gonna get something to eat?" "I'm tired and in a bad mood Zavia, I'll grab you some food and drop you off?" "Ok", I said pissed off because I could have been eating in the cafeteria all this time.

As we drove towards my house, I could feel the stress emanating from Reece but I couldn't be bothered to talk to him. He had acted like a spoilt brat and I wasn't going to get embroiled in a discussion with him. Better to wait until he was calm. He pulled up outside New Thriving restaurant and went inside to order. After about ten minutes, he came back and handed me a bag of food which smelt amazing. "Sorry I'm in a bad mood baby, I'll be fine after I get some sleep." "That's cool", I said and reached for his hand. We continued the drive in silence but it was now comfortable rather than tense. When we got to my house, I leant over to kiss him and he returned my chaste kiss by grabbing my hair and kissing me passionately probing my mouth with his tongue. I was startled by his fervour. Then just as I was starting to enjoy it, he pulled away from me and said: "I'm sorry Zavia that was too much". "No, it wasn't," I assured him. "Didn't you enjoy it? Don't you want more sometimes? Don't you want to make love to me?" "Yes?" he said. He looked at my lips, slowly chewing his own and said "I can't believe that you have to ask that. You must know that I want you more than ever, but we have to wait until we're married. It's not long". "I guess so", I replied, disappointed that he wasn't even going to discuss it with me. "Anyway, you better go before the food gets cold", he said. "I love you Zavi, see you tomorrow. Do you need me to take you to UG?" "No, I don't", I said. "I'll mostly be working at Jupiter Press. The owner's daughter is in my group." "Ok cool", he said.

After dinner, I went straight to bed and slept until the next morning when my alarm went off at 6.30am. I got up and did my chores, and prepared Lucky for nursery before I went to meet the team at Jupiter Press. It was within walking distance from my house so I took my time getting ready. As I walked through the gates of Jupiter Press, the security guard asked for my name. I told him and explained the purpose of my visit. While I waited for him to verify my details Nicholas came up behind me and volunteered his name as well.

"How are you this morning?" I said, "I'm good thanks," he said "glad that we won yesterday's game despite your brother's best efforts". "My brother?" I said looking confused. "Adam wasn't on the court yesterday." "Adam? Who's Adam? I'm talking about Reece." "Reece? He's not my brother" I said "he's my fiancé". Nicholas looked at me in surprise just as the security guard came back to the window and gave us passes. As we thanked him and walked in Nicholas said "back to what we were saying, that guy Reece is your fiancé? Wow, I never even noticed the ring on your finger. Aren't you a bit too young to get married?" "Well we aren't getting married until next year when I'll be 18," I said, "it isn't going to change my future plans just my name". "If you say so", he said, "I expected you to be more the independent career woman type". "Why would you say that?" I said. "Because you have incredible vision and you're a natural leader." I blushed slightly and said "thanks, but you don't know Reece or me that well. Reece will support all of my ambitions, he has already suggested that I go into politics. I will be just fine with him". "Cool," he said shrugging.

As we got into the office, we found Jake already there with his shoulders hunched over a notebook. "Hey Jake," I said. "Have you seen Anna?" "Yes, she just went to get some draft posters for you guys to see before she puts them up around UG". "Thanks", I said. "So what ideas have you got for the fashion show Nicholas?" "I thought we could get sponsorship and clothes from boutiques and stalls in the markets. We also need to find some models." "That bit is easy," I said, "there are lots of girls who want to model. We used a few at my school fair last year". "Cool", he said. "Let's start making calls." And that became our routine, meeting at Jupiter Press and working together companionably.

Two weeks passed and we found ourselves only a week and a half away from the Fashion Show. Nicholas and I worked well together and had found a nice rhythm. As usual, on a Monday morning, we met at Jupiter Press. Our first appointment was at 1pm that day so after a morning making calls we gathered our papers and caught a taxi into the centre of town. We were meeting Nicholas's stepmother's friend who ran a local shoe shop and as we sat in the taxi, we discussed strategy and agreed that Nicholas would lead. The meeting went well. Nicholas was charming and had our contact eating out of his hand. We agreed on shoe donations for all the girls and left feeling pleased with ourselves. "I'm starving", said Nicholas "Let's grab something to eat before our next meeting". "Good idea" I replied. "There's a place near here that does amazing food. I'll show you." We wove through the back streets near Stabroek Market where our next meeting would be and arrived in front of Tastees a popular restaurant renowned for its range of food. Once we were inside, we looked around for an empty table and a waiter signalled for us to try upstairs. I followed Nicholas up the stairs and was relieved to see some spare tables. Menus were already on the table so we grabbed them and sat silently poring over them trying to decide what to eat.

I made my selection and glanced up to see Reece's cousin Portia walk in. I put my head down hoping she wouldn't notice me but it was too late. She waved and walked towards us. "So who's your friend Zavia," she said, in a fake voice barely concealing her contempt for me. I didn't like her very much but as one of Reece's favourite cousins I had to tolerate her. "This is Nicholas", I said, "he's part of my project team on the UG programme". "Oh cool", she said "It figures that you met him through school. There can't be many guys dumb enough to try to compete with my cousin for someone like you." I cut my eyes on her, but she had already turned her attention to Nicholas. "Hey, Nicholas. Nice to meet you", she said flirtatiously. I rolled my eyes behind my menu and watched as she surveyed him like a prime piece of meat. "I can't believe I've never met you. Which school do you go to?" "I go to boarding school in Berbice", he said. "I'm only in town for the holidays and even then it's usually just briefly before I fly out somewhere." "Oh, that explains it. There's no way I would have missed a fine specimen like you! Anyway, I gotta go" she said. "Get my number from Zavia" and with that, she was gone in a haze of perfume and twisty hips.

"How do you know her?" said Nicholas. "She seems very high maintenance". "She's Reece's cousin" I replied, "Didn't you hear her mention her cousin?" "No, can't say I did. I wasn't paying much attention to her rambling, but her being Reece's cousin explains a lot." I decided not to respond or question what he meant and luckily for me a waitress came to take our orders so I didn't have to. We ordered our food and as soon as it arrived, we hungrily wolfed it down.

When I looked at my watch, it was almost 3.30pm. "We need to go", I said, "we're meeting Mr Singh the textile stall owner soon". Our meeting with Mr Singh was also a success and we were happy with what we had achieved in a day. As it was already half past four, I didn't go back to the office. Any other calls I wanted to make I could do from home. I bid Nicholas farewell and made my way home, glad to be in a little bit early so that I could relax.

When I got in, I grabbed a drink and the phone and took them to my room. I sat at my desk making calls for an hour until Adam called out to say that Reece had just pulled up outside. I skipped down the stairs and stepped onto the porch taking a seat on the bench outside waiting for him to park. When he got to the steps, he said, "I thought we could go out to dinner to make up for yesterday". "I'm sorry Reece, I had a big lunch and I've got studying to do." He looked annoyed like a spoilt child. "What did you have for lunch?" "I went to Tastees and had soup." "Who did you go with?" he said looking at me. "I went with Nicholas from UG." "Nicholas?" he said, "as in Nicky from the basketball court?" "Yes", I said, "we're on the same project team". "You know, when Portia called and told me she saw you in Tastees with a guy I actually didn't believe her. I can't believe you're out there going on lunch dates with the guy who tried to humiliate me on the court." "Oh please Reece, I haven't got time for this I wasn't on a date with him, we had lunch between meetings." "Well, I don't want you spending time with him. It doesn't look good for me having my fiancée having lunch with another man". "Oh, so I can't choose my friends now?" I said. "No, not if they aren't my friends too" he shouted. "Wow," I growled. "Did you really just say that?" "Yes, I did" Reece replied belligerently. "Well, you know what? You need to go and think about that position and get back to me when you calm down." "Fine," he said through gritted teeth as he flounced down the stairs and out of the yard.

He was such a brat sometimes I thought as I went upstairs to take a shower. I got to the landing and bumped into Adam, "how come it's so quiet around here?" "Mum and Dad have taken Lucky and JoJo to get ice cream as a treat and they aren't back yet". "Cool", I said glad that I would have more time in the shower. I went into the bathroom and turned the shower on, setting it to hot and feeling it pound against my body. Because no one had been home for most of the day, I got a steady stream of hot water and I felt rejuvenated as I stepped out. Just as I was drying myself, Adam knocked and said "phone for you Zavia". "Ok," I said "leave it on my bed, I'll be out in a minute". "Cool," he said.

I took my time drying my skin thinking that Reece could just wait until I was good and ready. After a couple of minutes, I went into my room and picked up the phone closing the door and sitting on my bed. "Calling to apologise huh?" "Apologise for what?" said an unfamiliar voice. "Who is this?" I said. "It's Nicholas" "Oh", I said "hi". "Hi to you too. So who is it that needs to apologise to you?" "No one," I said. "So to what do I owe the pleasure of this call?" "Well, I've managed to arrange a meeting at the Sports Hall tomorrow morning to finalise the arrangements for the fashion show, so I wanted to see if you could meet me there at 9am?" "Sure," I said, "no problem, do you want to meet up beforehand?" "No, it's cool I live about five minutes away from the Sports Hall so I'll meet you there."

The next morning, I dressed for a business meeting and arrived at the Sports Hall a little bit early, Nicholas was already there sitting in the cafe having some orange juice. "Hi", I said slipping into the booth next to him. "Hey", he replied. As he turned, I noticed that he had a moustache of orange juice on his top lip. I picked up a tissue and wiped his face. As I wiped his mouth, he stared at me intently and as I made contact with his skin, I felt a jolt. I pulled my hand away and stuttered an apology struggling to maintain eye contact with him. "Thanks" he murmured staring at me. "It's ok", I said. Before I was forced to deal with how my stomach was churning a member of staff came over and said: "Mr Clifton can see you now". "Fantastic," I said jumping up quickly.

We went in to talk to Mr Clifton. He was incredibly supportive and really did like our vision. However, he wanted to double check some details with his events manager who wouldn't be in until after lunch so he told us to come back in two hours. As we left, we felt jubilant, but having to hang around for two hours with nowhere to work or make calls from seemed like a waste. "We can go to my house if you want?" Said Nicholas. "I live five minutes away and we have an office at the house that we can use today because my mum has a day off." Hmm, I thought. I didn't want to further infuriate Reece but frankly, we had work to do.

As we walked towards Nicholas' house, I asked him what his mother did. He explained that she was a designer and owned a boutique in town. "Which boutique?" I said "Nicolette's" he replied. "Wow, your mum is Nicolette? That makes sense. I mean you're called Nicholas. Will she be home? I'd love to meet her. Now I understand how you have the boutique contacts for the fashion show. Will she be giving us stuff?" All my sentences rolled into one as I was excited to meet her. "I don't know yet," he said. "She wants to meet you first." "Meet me? Why me?" "Because you're the team leader", he said. "She wants to see what and who she would be investing in." "Ok", I said, "If she is home I guess it's a good opportunity to convince her".

When we got to his house, I was impressed to see a ranch style building that looked like it belonged in Dallas. It was beautiful red brick and all I kept thinking was that this was my idea of a dream house. We walked up the driveway and the door was opened by a short matronly woman. "Hi, Marguerite," he said, "is Mum home?" "No Nicky she isn't," she said. "This is Marguerite," said Nicholas "and this is Zavia, my friend". Marguerite proffered her hand and I shook it daintily. "She is very lovely Nicky". "I know," he said, "but she is my boss at the moment so no business and pleasure". Marguerite laughed and said, "are you going into the living room?" "No", he said, "we're going to go use the office". "Ok", she said, "I'm going back to the kitchen to sort out dinner, remember your grandparents are coming over tonight so you need to be home by 6pm". "I know, I know Mags," he said giving her a kiss and she swatted him away.

"Follow me Zavia," he said as Marguerite retreated to the rear of the house. I followed him along a corridor. He unlocked a door into an amazing dining room which had French doors that opened out onto a well maintained lawn. We walked through the dining room and French doors towards another building at the end of the property. "I thought we were going to the office?" I said. "We are" he replied rolling his eyes. "You're very impatient aren't you?" I snorted and said "whatever."

As we got to the office, I noticed a security hut next to the building, Nicholas waved at the woman who was sitting in the hut and called out "is it open?" "Yes", she said, "your mother has only popped out for a couple of hours so she couldn't be bothered to lock it all up". "Good", he said. When we got to the door, he turned the handle and pushed it open. The first thing that struck me was the coolness of the air conditioning. The next thing that hit me was the size of the office. We were standing in a room with four desks, a large copier, filing cabinets and numerous other doors. "I thought you said your mum had an office," I murmured, "this is a whole complex". He smiled and said, "I think you'll find that office does adequately describe this but let me do the grand tour". We walked through the office which had a kitchenette, bathroom including a shower, the desks I had noticed earlier and a stationery room. I thought it was fantastic.

"Now you know where everything is, let's get down to work," Nicholas said "pick a desk. Have you got all the numbers we need?" "Yes", I said. We worked steadily for an hour making phone calls and making faces at each other while we worked. We were a good team and I enjoyed our natural rhythm and way of dividing up things to do. As I was finishing another successful sponsorship call, I heard an insistent buzzing. "What's that?" I said as Nicholas got up and walked towards the door. "It's the intercom," he said "it's linked to the house. Hey", he said as he pressed a button "Hey to you too" I heard a young sounding female voice answer. "Where are you?" "I'm in the office," he said. "Cool, I'll see you in a minute. I'm bringing you a treat". I felt a sudden stab of jealousy. "Was that your girlfriend?" I said stiffly. Nicholas turned and said, "yeah that's my girl" and smiled. I felt irrationally upset by his response but braced myself to be all smiles with this girl. I didn't even know why I felt jealous, I had Reece and it wasn't as if Nicholas had given me any indication that he didn't have a girlfriend. I busied myself with some papers while surreptitiously glancing at the door awaiting the arrival of the girlfriend.

Unfortunately, the phone rang just as the door flew open so I couldn't focus all my attention on assessing Nicholas' taste in women. As I stared intently at the door while trying to talk to the jewellery supplier, I was shocked to see Nicolette float into the room. She was carrying a tray of snacks and some drinks and she smiled brightly at me and gave Nicholas a kiss as she entered the office. She oozed effortless style and sophistication from her oversized sunglasses to her flat sandals and bohemian summer dress. I already felt self-conscious in my sensible linen dress that I had chosen to wear for our business meetings that day.

As I clicked the phone off, having secured some key pieces for sale at the fashion show, Nicholas turned and said: "Mum this is Zavia, the girl I was telling you about". "Aaah Zavia," she said. "Finally, I get to meet the person with such a unique name. Nicky has been raving on about you for the past couple of days. Somehow I assumed you were a tomboy who would be dressed in basketball clothes." "Mum" Nicholas growled "don't make it sound like I talk about her all the time. You're making me sound like a stalker". "If the cap fits" she muttered with a smile.

"So Zavia, Nicky tells me that you want some outfits for your fashion show. I won't just give them to you because Nicky is my son.

Tell me why I should support you guys." "No problem," I replied. "The aim of our business is to increase awareness of your brand amongst the younger generation. Guyana is a society of new money and entrepreneurial spirit is high. This means that to cultivate brand loyalty you have to engage with the consumers at an earlier stage than is usual. I believe that your brand should be one of our key partners. The sponsorship package would involve you providing us with samples that we will take orders on. For every order made through us, we would earn commission. Other partners on board include Flowers on Main Street, Eye Spy the sunglass specialists and Preeti Patel, the makeup artist".

"Wow", she said "I like her Nicky. She has style and strong business acumen. Incidentally, how did you get Preeti on board? She is notoriously hard to convince". "Nicholas negotiated our deal with her," I said, "he charmed her into a meeting over the telephone then closed the deal with her over coffee". "You two make a good team. I'll be happy to come on board," said Nicolette. "Fabulous," I replied and walked over to Nicholas to give him a high five.

We now had four out of our five chosen sponsors on board. "Speaking of sponsors. Mum, we need to go back to the Sports Hall to confirm the venue deal with Mr Clifton". "Ok honey", she said, "Zavia can you ensure that I have a written agreement for our arrangement by the end of the week?" "Yes of course," I said, "great to meet you". "You too, oh and don't forget your snacks. Drop them into your bag in case you get hungry later today" she said. "Oh yes". In my excitement, I had forgotten the snacks she had brought in earlier.

As we walked out through the gates, I felt like I was floating on air. "Can you believe we've secured nearly all our sponsors? We do make a fantastic team" I said. "So if that's the case how's about you ditch your fiancé and go on a date with me?" Nicholas said. "Erm, I can't ..." I started to stutter thinking *why the hell did he say that*. Before I could go on justifying why I wouldn't be ditching Reece he said "Just kidding!" and I punched him on the arm.

That afternoon we got the agreement for the venue and suddenly it was as if everything fell into place all at once. The team was doing well planning the Fashion Show and my personal issues with Reece had calmed down. He hadn't apologised but little by little we had returned to our routine and he didn't ask much about my project so the arguments stopped.

As the date of the Fashion Show drew closer, my schedule got more and more hectic and Nicholas and I found ourselves working late almost every night. The night the before the show we were doing last minute accessorising of outfits at my house with Zee and Adam giving us a hand. The four of us were messing around in the family room sorting through outfits and bagging shoes and accessories while listening to music. It was a nice vibe and Adam and Nicholas got on really well even though Adam had chosen Environmental Studies so wasn't at the university placement with us. Suddenly we heard the doorbell chiming over the music but because we were surrounded by clothes, shoes and jewellery none of us moved to get it. Nicholas and I were engrossed in comparing notes to find a pair of missing shoes. "You must have assigned them to the wrong person," I said. "No, I didn't," he replied. "Yes you did, let me see?" I said and leant over his shoulder scanning his list.

Just as I moved my hand to skim a line across his list, I heard someone clearing their throat and turned to find Reece standing at the door. "Enjoying yourself, are you Zavia? Is this why you've been ignoring the phone? Having too much fun with Nicky, are you?" I felt Nicholas stiffen and I said "no Reece we're working. Can't you see the four of us are knee deep in clothes?" "All I see is my fiancée leaning up on some other guy". "Don't be silly," I said, "We're just comparing notes". Nicholas shook his head and moved from next to me while muttering "ain't no one got no time for this bullshit". "What did you say?" said Reece belligerently. "Reece! what's the matter with you?" I interrupted. "What's the matter with me Zavia? What's wrong with you? I want to marry you and you're there flaunting yourself with other guys. I need you to act more like a wife."

Zee was looking from me to Reece with her jaw slightly slackened and a perplexed look on her face. I understood how she felt because I had never seen this side of Reece. He was behaving insecure and chauvinistic. "Let's go upstairs and talk," I said to Reece. He stood at the door glaring at Nicholas while I climbed over piles of clothes until I was next to him. I was so glad that Adam hadn't intervened because his temper could get out of hand, fast! As I walked through the door and softly closed it behind me, I grabbed Reece's arm before he could walk up the stairs. "What the fuck are you doing, acting like that? I've never given you a reason to doubt my commitment to you and all of a sudden you keep questioning me". "It's not you Zavi," he murmured. "It's that guy. He rubs me up the wrong way. He is a cocky asshole and I don't want him getting too close to you and giving people the wrong impression." "Well, I think I can handle myself." I retorted still angry about the way that he had behaved. "I know Zavia, it's just you know how much I love you and I want to protect you." "I know," I said. "Well, the placement is over tomorrow and then all you have to do is see him next week for your assessment session then you never need to see him again." "I guess," I said wondering why my heart felt so heavy at the thought of not seeing Nicholas anymore.

"Ok, well I need to go and finish. What did you need?" I said. "Nothing, I just wanted to check in on you," said Reece "I was just passing before I go to pick up my grandmother. I'll see you tomorrow at the show," he said. "Yep", I said and as I turned to walk away, he grabbed me and gave me a lingering kiss, squeezing my butt with one hand and letting his other hand rub my stomach, chest and breasts. As I melted into his kiss, he released me and said "gotta go" and walked away, leaving me feeling cold and a little confused.

The atmosphere was different when I went back into the room and for a full five minutes, no one said a word. Then Zee said, "wow that whole vow of chastity seems to have Reece wound up a little tightly don't you think Zavia?" "What vow of chastity?" said Nicholas and I looked at Zee in disbelief not quite comprehending that she had just shamelessly let out one of my biggest secrets. "Oh, yeah," said Adam to Nicholas, "Zavia and Reece have never actually had sex. He's taken a vow of celibacy until they're married". "How do you know that Adam?" I asked incredulously. "Zee, did you tell him?" "Nah Dad told me after the engagement party. He was drunk and blurted it out when we were locking up the house that night" Adam replied. Nicholas raised his eyebrows and said "no way" and Adam laughed and said "Yep, hand on heart that boy is a virgin". Nicholas shook his head and said, "huh! Interesting!". Luckily my humiliation lessened the tension in the room and we were able to regain some of the fun of our earlier session. As it approached midnight, Zee said she needed to go home and Adam offered to take her. "Thanks for helping Zee," I said. "Nicholas and I can finish off here. We're pretty much done anyway". "Great," Adam said "let me get my shoes. I'll be upstairs when you're ready Zee". "Thanks, Ads," said Zee. "See you tomorrow Zavia. I'll be there at 5pm for my fittings and makeup", she said. "Thanks, Zee see you in the morning."

Now it was just Nicholas and me, the tension returned to the room so I hummed quietly to myself. The music was off because it was too late to play it and the silence was deafening. "Zavia, are you really not sleeping with that guy?" "Wow", I said, "that was to the point and kinda none of your business". "I know, but I'm asking". "No, I haven't slept with him. Why? Do I look like a hoe or something?" "No, it's not that," he said hesitantly. "Whoa, why did you hesitate?" I said. "Because I've heard rumours about you?" he replied. "You've had some popular boyfriends and now you're with Reece. It seems unrealistic that you would be a virgin". "Well, I am," I snarled as I walked over to him and poked him in the chest. "What kind of person asks me such a personal question and then refutes the answer? Anyone would think that you had fucked me you seem so sure". "No honey, not me. Definitely not me." He said it with such contempt that I raised my hand to slap him, but he grabbed me and said "do not push me Zavia. You may regret it." "Regret what?" I spat out "you don't scare me". "Well I should," he said. "Why?" I said belligerently. I felt tired and annoyed and ready to fight with anyone. "Don't push me Zavia," he repeated. "Or what?" I said, "or what?" "Or this!" He said and crushed his lips against mine. At first, I pushed him away shocked at what he had done but as it became apparent that my pushing was futile, I surrendered to the kiss. I opened my mouth and accepted his tongue as it probed my mouth. He expertly played with my tongue, stroking in and out of my mouth with a rhythm reminiscent of the few times that Reece had fingered me. I could feel the familiar stirring between my legs and my nipples puckered up.

I didn't even notice that he was no longer holding my wrists and that I was willingly participating. I had on a short summer dress and he slowly moved his hands to rub his rough palms against my arms. Although not an intimate movement it felt more intimate than anything I had ever experienced with anyone else. He hugged me close to him and ran his hands down my back clasping my buttocks under the thin cotton material. All too soon he pulled his mouth away from mine. I looked at him blinking as if my eyes needed to get re-accustomed to the light, but he wasn't done. Within a minute, he was kissing my neck while continuing to squeeze my buttocks. I moaned enjoying the feeling of his mouth on my neck. His hands rubbed more insistently and he slowly bunched up my dress so it was riding higher and higher. Suddenly like an electric shock, I felt his rough hands make contact with my skin, their roughness meeting the softness of my butt cheeks. He guided me towards the sofa and just as we were about to sink into it I heard footsteps coming towards the door. I jumped away from him smoothing my dress as quickly as I could.

Adam bounded into the room unaware of what he had interrupted. "Zee's home safe and I'm going to a party at the Sports Hall so I thought I'd offer you a lift home, Nicholas". "Oh, great," said Nicholas "let's go. You'll be ok with the last bits won't you Zavia?" "Err, yes, I'll be all right," I said, my mind still reeling from the kiss. I felt very confused. Nicholas was very different to Reece. Reece represented growing up and restrictions whereas Nicholas represented freedom and passion. What a predicament! And to top it off Nicholas was acting like nothing had happened. Maybe Reece was right, he was an asshole.

I barely slept that night tossing and turning, partly due to nerves because of the Fashion Show but also because of my encounter with Nicholas. Suddenly all the doubts that I had about getting married to Reece had returned with a vengeance and I wondered whether I would indeed be able to chase my dreams while being Mrs Reece Rodrigues. All too soon the sun cracked through my window and I had to get up. First stop of the day was the hairdresser; I had a 9am appointment so I jumped out of bed, into the shower and quickly made my way to Miss Simone's. When my hair was done, I went to the Sports Hall to decorate. Jake and Anna were there but Nicholas wasn't and I was glad. "Where's Nicholas?" I said. "he was here, but he's gone to help Preeti and he's collecting the flowers for the models," said Anna. "Cool," I said glad that I would be delaying seeing him because I wasn't sure how I felt.

As I set up the makeshift dressing rooms, I saw Reece's car turn into the car park. I continued to set up waiting for him to get out of the car and come to help me or speak to me, but instead he sat in his car watching me. Because of the distance, he was away from me, I knew he couldn't tell that I had seen him and I wondered what was taking him so long. "Anna come and help me put up this dividing curtain," I said. As she bound over with her usual excitement and energy, she said, "does your fiancé always stop by to watch you?" "What do you mean?" I said. "Well he's been sitting in the car park for the last ten minutes and now he's gone". I turned around and saw that she was right; Reece's car was no longer in the car park. I couldn't believe that he would check up on me. Thankfully Nicholas wasn't here and I had been by myself so no doubt he was content.

By 3pm, the venue was set up. Nicholas had come in with the flowers and had worked on the other side of the room, waving to me when he arrived but making no attempt to speak to me. I felt annoyed and confused, but I was so busy I didn't get the chance to dwell on it. Once finished, I packed up my things and called out to Anna that I was going home to sort out the outfits and get dressed. As I banged into the house, I found Adam and all his friends waiting for me. They had volunteered to move the outfits from our basement to the Sports Hall for me. I had half an hour to help them load up and then Anna would meet them on the other side to put everything into the relevant dressing rooms. As I was helping load Adam's car, my mum came outside with the cordless phone, "it's Reece" she said. "Hey," I said breathlessly. "Why do you sound breathless?" he asked sharply. Somehow even such a simple question irritated me. "I'm loading clothes into Adam's car" I responded equally sharply. "Oh cool, what time do you need to be back at the Sports Hall?" "By 4.30pm," I said. "Ok well, I'll take you if you want". "That would be great," I said. "but listen, let me finish loading up and getting ready. I'll see you soon". "Ok, babe," he said and hung up. As the last outfit went into the car, I breathed a sigh of relief and ran into the house to take another shower. I showered in lightning time and then ran into my bedroom to dress. I needed to look good. I wasn't modelling, but it only meant that I had to make more of an effort.

I sprayed myself with perfume and stepped into my dress, calling out to my mum, asking her to help me zip it up. As she stood behind me in front of the mirror she smiled and said: "you look beautiful, you should think of a similar cut for your wedding dress". I stiffened and she asked, "what's wrong Zavia?" "Nothing," I said brightly trying to cover the feeling of rising panic she had caused by her comment. "I'm just a bit nervous about tonight." "Oh you'll be okay," she said, "I'm sorry I can't be there. You know I would have loved to be, but I'm looking after Lucky and JoJo. Your dad and Uncle Compton will be there rooting for you, though." "I know," I said. "Thanks for zipping me up." "Not a problem" she replied as she left the room.

I quickly packed my clutch bag with lipstick, tissues and mints and made my way downstairs with my shoes in my hand. The heels were so high I had no intentions of putting them on until just before the show started so I was wearing leather flip flops. Reece still hadn't arrived so I went to the kitchen for a drink. As I stuck my head into the fridge trying to decide what juice to pick, I felt little arms snake around me. "Hey, Lucky," I said without turning. I knew that it would be my baby brother. No one else was that small or capable of sneaking up on me. "ZavZav," he said and as I turned, I noticed that he had an empty cup in his hand and I laughed. I took the cup out of his hand and filled it. First I took a large mouthful then held it to his mouth. We stood in the kitchen alternating mouthfuls until it was almost finished. Just as I was holding it to Lucky's mouth for the last time, my mum walked in and said "aah Zavia, you know he isn't supposed to have undiluted juice. You spoil him too much" he smiled at me with a twinkle in his eyes and I smiled back at him with an identical twinkle.

Before my mother could continue her lecture on the evils of sugar I heard the doorbell. "That must be Reece," I said gratefully. I kissed my mother on the cheek and gave Lucky a kiss and a hug and ran to the door. "Walk Zavia, you're in a dress" my mum shouted at me and I rolled my eyes. Reece stood at the door in shorts and a t-shirt. "How come you're not dressed?" I said to him as we got into the car. "I'm only dropping you off," he said. "Then I need to run a couple of errands for my grandmother. I'll be at the Sports Hall by about 7.30pm, 8pm at the latest".

Sometimes I was thoroughly irritated by Reece's devotion to his grandmother and this was one of those times. What had appeared sweet when we first met now felt like an intrusion. As his fiancée, he should have been helping me tonight, not running after her but I kept all these thoughts to myself and said "ok" petulantly. "No point acting like a brat about it Zavia. Who else is going to help Granny?" My temper flared and I narrowed my eyes at him "I'm not a brat" I said, "I just assumed you were going to help me with the last minute stuff". "Well, I'm not," he said "and I didn't say I was, so you can only blame yourself for your assumptions". I shrugged my shoulders but didn't say anything more. We sat in silence for the remainder of the journey both of us lost in our thoughts.

As we pulled up at the Sports Hall, Reece said: "Anyway you've got Nicky to help you". "I guess I do," I said as I slammed the door of his car and walked away. At this point, I didn't care if he came back or not I just needed to cool down and get my emotions in check so that I could focus on the Fashion Show. I got to the stage area, dropped off my bag and went to find Anna. My arrival meant that she could go home and change.

She quickly ran through all the models who had already checked in and handed me the clipboard with all the logistics. Considering how ditzy she seemed, she was incredibly focused and I was glad that we had worked together. As we were going through everything, Jake came over and said: "you ready Anna?" I looked at him quizzically and Anna smiled and said: "Jake and I are dating." "Wow," I said, "you two are dark horses aren't you?" "Yea, I guess it's true that opposites attract" Jake said smiling. "Nicholas should be back in about ten minutes and we'll be back by 6.30pm". "Perfect," I said. Still amused that they were dating.

I took the clipboard and went round to the room that we had set up for makeup. Preeti was there listening to music and drinking beer. "Hey Preeti," I said. "Thanks again for doing this for us." "No problem," she said "Nicholas is quite the charmer. If I were a couple of years younger, I'd be trying to get his attention". I laughed and said, "I bet you would". Laughing she continued and said "I've done all the girls who are here. I'll stay during the show to do touch ups and change colouring to match outfits as well". "That's perfect," I said "and in return, we have created these fliers to advertise your services". "Great," she said, "Nicholas showed me the proof and I was really impressed with them". "Do you want me to do your makeup?" she said. "I don't wear makeup" I replied. "Really?" she said, "well you're the first girl I've met in a long time who doesn't wear makeup. Come over here to the light and I'll give you a mini makeover if you want." "Ok", I said and sat down. "Wow, you have amazing eyelashes!" she said. "Thanks", I said. For the next ten minutes, she busied herself while I sat as still as a statue. When she was finished, she stood back to admire her work, clapped her hands delightedly and said "all done!" before handing me a mirror. When I looked in the mirror, it was like looking at someone else. The way that Preeti had done my eyes made them look narrower, yet more open and she had matched the turquoise of my dress perfectly.

I smiled at her and said "Thanks, Preeti" and she said "it's fine. It was a pleasure, you have flawless skin. I don't often work with such a beautiful blank canvas." I blushed and she said "hey when you blush you mess up my colour palette" and we laughed.

As we laughed the door opened and Nicholas came in with the last four models. "Here you go Preeti, your final four. Who's that in the chair?" He asked confused, as I had my back to him. "I don't remember turquoise being one of our colours tonight." I jumped off the stool and turned to face him. "Wow", he said staring at me, "you look beautiful Zavia". Preeti stood watching him look at me. I felt self-conscious as we stared deeply into each other's eyes. All too soon the spell was broken by Juanita one of the models. She came in and linked her arm through Nicholas' and said "you know what? I'll do my makeup later. Nicky take me to see my outfits". Nicholas looked shell shocked and continued to stare at me while Juanita physically pulled him out of the room by his arm.

Preeti laughed as they left the room and whispered "Wow, looks like I wouldn't have had a chance with him considering how he feels about you. Poor Juanita's putting up a good fight, though". "nothing is going on with Nicholas and I. I don't even know if we are friends. I guess we're colleagues" I said soberly. "Yea whatever Zavia," she said, "we'll see". "Well, I better be going," I said, "I have lots to do". I went to check in on the other models and bumped into Nicholas as I was making my way towards the ticket hall to give them sample tickets. "I'll walk with you," said Nicholas. "So are we going to talk about the other night?" he said. "What do you want to say about it?" I said. "Well, Zavia, you must know I like you." "I guess," I said, "I didn't really think too much about it". "Oh okay, well I thought about it a lot and I enjoyed it. But the reality is that you're getting married to Reece". "Well, it's not like you're not involved with someone too" I retorted. "Involved with who?" he replied looking confused. "Juanita," I said drily. "Nah, I'm not with Juanita. We've hooked up a couple of times when I've been home during the holidays, but she isn't my girl or anything". "Oh right, you've hooked up?" "Yes, Zavia we've hooked up". "Ok well, it's none of my business," I said and he looked at me strangely and said, "I guess it isn't".

We got to the ticket hall and quickly ran through all the admission arrangements, they also issued us with four walkie-talkies so that our team could communicate with each other. "Are you excited?" I said to Nicholas, trying to change the subject. "Yea, I guess I am," he said, "but I've been around the buzz of shows before so I'm kinda immune to it. I grew up with Nicolette remember?" "Oh yes," I said "and because she's a single mum I was always at her shows" he continued. "Oh, I didn't know your mum was a single mum. I guess I always assume everyone lives with their mum and dad because I do and all of my friends do". "Well, they don't," he said, "my dad is a married man who lives in America. His wife never had children and he had an affair with Nicolette when she was young. He and his wife visit every couple of years and I spend time with them or I go to see him every other Summer. It's unconventional, but it works". "I guess so," I said surprised to hear about such an arrangement. "My mum would have killed my dad if he had brought another child into the family and I can imagine my older siblings would have had quite a lot to say as well".

"Let's do a quick time check," said Nicholas closing the conversation about his family. "It's now 6pm, we have an hour until curtains up. We've made all the entry arrangements and all the girls are made up. They've all been given their outfits and from 6.30pm Anna and Jake are going to be backstage taking care of everything. Our job will be to troubleshoot during the show and then when it's the after party we can relax. On that note, I have a surprise for you. We aren't hosting tonight; our host is Sean Jacobson". "Sean Jacobson?" I said, "the radio, DJ? How the hell did you swing that?" "He's my godfather," he said, "he and Nicolette grew up together". "Wow", I said, "you're a dark horse". "I thought you would like it" he murmured. "I do," I said. "Good because Sean is due to arrive in about ten minutes and we need to brief him using our notes."

"I'm nervous," I said, getting breathless. Nicholas turned to me and said, "you're serious aren't you?" "Yes. I'm nervous," I said strangling out another breath. He laughed and squeezed my hand saying "don't be nervous. This is our night. You're going to be fabulous and it will be amazing". I smiled at him and said "Thank you" before disentangling my hand feeling slightly self-conscious by the physical contact. "Right, let's grab some juice while we wait for Sean. I told him to meet us at the bar" Nicholas said. "Great," I said, "I'm thirsty and I doubt I'll be able to drink anything once we start working". We sat down and ordered cherry juices. "I love cherry juice. It's the tastiest juice known to man" I said. Nicholas sniggered and said, "I'm sure that some juices taste infinitely sweeter". Something about the way he said it made me blush and then giggle "whatever" I said and he smiled.

As I was doing a final read-through of the notes for Sean, I looked up to ask Nicholas something and noticed his eyes looking past me. I turned to see what he was looking at and saw Sean Jacobson walking into the Sports Hall. He walked with an air of confidence and the women at the Admissions Hall all stopped what they were doing to observe him and he rewarded them with a big wave and thousand-watt smile. "Some of them look like they're going to pass out," I said drily and Nicholas sniggered and said, "trust me I've seen that happen before". As Sean approached our table, Nicholas got up to greet him and I stood as well not wanting to appear rude to our guest DJ.

Sean enveloped Nicholas in a big bear hug and said: "how's my favourite godson doing today". "I'm good," said Nicholas "bearing in mind you saw me last night when you were at Mum's for dinner". "Yea whatever, those are just details," said Sean. "You always have to be the smart guy." Nicholas smiled back at him just as he turned and said: "Is this the girl that your mum told me about?" I raised my eyebrows at Nicholas and he shrugged and said: "I wouldn't know what Mum said to you because I wasn't a part of the conversation". "She told me about a gorgeous and smart young lady you brought to the house who would make a perfect girlfriend for you if you bothered to settle down and see what was staring you in the face". I gulped and blushed furiously. "Whatever man", said Nicholas. "This is Zavia, she's smart and she's my business partner." "Pleased to meet you Zavia," said Sean. "How old are you?" "I'm 17," I said quizzically. "Damn," he said," if you were only a year older we could have been having a very different conversation". "Wow", I said with my eyes wide open "did you really just say that to me?" "Yes, he did," said Nicholas. "Aaah don't take me seriously sweetie. I was trying to get a rise out of Nicky, but apparently, that didn't work". "Oh ok whatever," I said, "shall we get down to business". Sean looked at Nicholas mischievously and I belatedly realised what I had said. I opened my mouth to protest but Nicholas shook his head and said: "Behave Sean. She's embarrassed enough". Sean turned and smiled at me and said: "Ok let's talk through what you need from me tonight".

I was grateful for the respite from his banter and soon fell into my flow of explaining the event and giving him his cues and prompts. I was extremely happy with the way the briefing had gone and when I looked at my watch it was almost 7pm. "It's almost show time," said Nicholas "let me take Sean to get wired up and you take the walkie-talkies to Jake and Anna". "Ok cool", I said "don't forget to take yours and have a great evening Sean". I said. "I'll see you in about half hour

Zavia" said Nicholas".

I walked towards the dressing area and found Jake and Anna already there calming some frayed nerves and giving the models pep talks. I eavesdropped on Jake and he was surprisingly soothing and calm as he spoke to the girls and put them at ease. The doors would open any minute now and the show would start at 7.30pm. I strolled back to the front of the Sports Hall and found lines of people already milling just outside the entrance, it looked like we would have a good turnout and I breathed a sigh of relief.

Two hours later I was standing backstage listening to Sean do the closing remarks and messages of appreciation to the models and our sponsors. The crowd was rapturous and at last count, we had exceeded our target number of orders. Our sponsors all looked happy and the technology hadn't failed us. Sean finally announced that the After-Party would be in the Main Hall and the crowd went wild. I hadn't seen Reece all night, but it occurred to me I had been so busy that I hadn't even really noticed. As the curtain fell, Nicholas grabbed me in a bear hug, lifted me off the ground and said "we did it Zavia! We did it!" "Did what?" I said. "Jake has just told me via the walkie-talkie that we took over $100,000 and there were over 50 items ordered. We've smashed all our targets!" He squeezed me tight and I whooped with joy. As he put me down, I saw Reece making his way over to us stony-faced.

"Get your hands off my fiancee," he said. Nicholas turned to him and I inserted myself between them remembering what had happened when they fought on the basketball court. "It's not what you think Reece," I said, upset that what had been a moment of jubilation was now being marred by Reece's jealousy. "Oh! My fiancée isn't made up like a French whore embracing another man? That isn't what I've seen? Is it?" I looked at him appalled at the fact he had called me a whore and instinctively my hand raised up and I delivered a stinging slap across his face. His eyes widened in shock and his hand lifted and I flinched, but he was just wiping a spot of blood from his lip which I had just burst. He didn't say another word to me. He shook his head and stormed out.

I stood there shaking with anger then burst into tears. The tears mingled with my makeup and I couldn't stop sobbing. Part of me knew it was partly adrenaline from the busy few weeks but it was also the embarrassment. Being called a whore in front of all these people had rocked me to the core. As I sobbed, Nicholas took my hand and led me outside. Anna and Jake followed him and Anna hugged me. "Listen take some time out Zavia. Jake and I can finish up here and we will see you at the After-Party". "Thank you", I said hugging her back tightly.

"Let's get out of here for awhile," said, Nicholas. As we moved through the crowd, I said: "where are we going?" "To my house, to calm you down" "Ok," I said numbly. On our way through the crowd we bumped into Zee and she said "I heard about what that asshole Reece said. Are you ok?" "Yes," I said, "But I need to get out of here for a while" she looked at Nicholas suspiciously as he stood protectively at my side. "I'll be okay Zee. I'm just going over to Nicholas' to sort my face out and chill, then I'll be back for the After-Party." "Ok", she said and then whispered something to Nicholas. As we walked away, I said, "what did she say?" "Nothing important," he said and we continued walking.

When we got to the Sports Hall exit gates, Nicolette was walking towards the car park with Sean. "Are you going home, Mum? We need a ride", said Nicholas. "Sean and I are going to Palm Court," she said, "but we can take you home first. Zavia are you ok?" "Yes", I muttered, "I'm just going to take Zavia home to clean her face and relax for a while then we will be back here until the early hours," Nicholas said. "Ok", his mum replied as we climbed into her jeep. It only took us five minutes to drive to Nicholas' and as we pulled up, I wondered what I was doing. I didn't even know him very well. As if reading my mind Nicolette leant back from the driver's seat, squeezed my hand and said "Nicky will take care of you. He has a kind heart and I'm sure you will feel better soon". Her kind words made tears well up in my eyes again and I wiped them away as she gave my hand one final squeeze.

Nicholas was holding my bag and he helped me out of the jeep before punching in the code to get through the gates. Nicolette tooted her horn as she drove back up the street and we strolled into the yard. As Nicholas opened the door, a light flicked on and I said: "I thought no one was home". "No one is home," he said, "it's a motion detector light that automatically comes on when the door is opened and there's no natural light". "That's cool," I whispered. "Yea I guess so," he said. "Let's go to the den," he said, "it's the cosiest room in the house". I slipped my shoes off and padded behind him as he led the way

72

towards the side of the house in a different direction to the one we had gone in when I had been there previously.

He opened a door and I found myself in a room with a big animal print rug on the floor and big sofas and a large TV. "I need to use the bathroom", I said, "my face must look a mess and I don't want to mess up the chairs". "Oh yeah, of course," he said, "Sorry, I'll show you and get you a towel". We left the room and he pointed me to a door further down the hall. "I'll pass you a towel in a second", he said. I went into the bathroom and found it was a large room that would have been more aptly named a powder room, it had large mirrors, a couple of upholstered stools and a toilet cubicle. I washed the streaks of makeup off my face gingerly and looked at myself in the mirror starting to cry all over again at Reece's cruel words. I also pulled my hair out of its side twist and left it to fall freely over my shoulders holding it off my face as I rinsed my eyes and cheeks.

Nicholas knocked on the door and said: "Can I come in?" "Yes, sure," I said. As he walked in, I turned to him and gazed into his eyes feeling like I was getting lost in a whirlpool. He moved my hair from my wet forehead and then as our eyes locked he leant towards me and I stepped closer meeting his lips with mine. We stood there kissing for what seemed like an eternity before his hands began exploring my body. He kissed me harder and harder and I threw my arms around his neck and pulled him towards me with ferocity. "Let's go back into the den," he said and I followed him meekly.

As soon as we were in the den, he kissed me again and guided me to one of the sofas. I sank into the sofa and said: "this feels like déjà vu". He smiled before devouring my mouth with an intensity that I had never experienced. We lay there with him on top of me kissing fervently and it felt like the most natural thing for me to undo his shirt to touch his chest. As my hand made contact with his chest he held it, looked at me and said "Zavia what are you doing to me? I find it very hard to control myself with you and you're only making it worse". "So why are you holding back?" I said. "You know why" he replied. "Well, I don't want you to," I said. "I've never felt this way and I don't want it to end," he looked at me and shook his head. "Zavia do you know what you're saying? You're supposed to be marrying Reece in a few months." I laughed sardonically and said "Yes I am and look at how he has treated me. You know what the old people always said, better to be judged by your deeds. So if he thinks I'm a whore, I may as well oblige." "You see that's just the thing Zavia. I don't want to be part of your revenge plot." "You're not, I promise you," I said, now sure more than ever about what I needed to do to make myself feel better and to rid myself of this wedding hanging over me like an albatross.

As Nicholas looked at me like a tortured soul, I took one of his fingers in my mouth and sucked on it while staring him dead in the eyes. "Stop" he whispered. "Zavia, stop!" But I didn't and I didn't break my stare. With an anguished moan, he got up and pulled me to stand up in front of him, kissing me while reaching behind me to unzip my dress. As it loosened, he pulled it down so that my bra was visible and massaged the top of my breasts while he kissed my neck. As his kisses moved slowly down my chest, he unclasped my bra, peeling it off my skin and freeing my breasts. He licked an outline around my aureoles causing my nipples to pucker and traced his fingers around my nipples. I felt a deep stirring in my groin and I moaned as his mouth followed his finger and he expertly sucked and teased my nipples. One at a time he took turns to nibble and suck them. I could feel my clitoris aching for attention, but I wasn't yet confident enough to tell him what I wanted. Instead, I rubbed my hands up and down his body finally mustering the courage to feel the bulge in his trousers which was pressing against my thigh. As I squeezed him through his trousers, he moaned and said: "Take it out". I had never done this before by myself, but I didn't want him to feel more apprehensive so I fumbled around with his belt and then felt my way to undo his button and unzip his trousers. As I rubbed his hardening penis, I could feel that his underwear was damp and I was surprised. "See what you've made me do already Zavia? You're incredibly sexy and you don't even know it. Do you?" I looked at him wide-eyed and he said: "You see, there it is, that look of pure innocence that makes me go weak at the knees".

As he said it, he held my face with both hands and kissed me deeply while using his body to push me back towards the sofa. As I fell onto the sofa, he broke our kiss and stepped backwards kicking off his trousers and shrugging out of his shirt. Once he was free, he took hold of my dress now near my knees and yanked it off. I was half sitting half lying in front of him in just my panties and I felt self-conscious. "Don't be shy baby," he said, "we are both in just our underwear".

I looked at him smiling hesitantly then boldly stood in front of him and pulled my panties down and off. A smile played on his lips as he returned the favour and then pushed me back onto the sofa and kissed me again. As he kissed me, he pressed against me and I moaned feeling a build-up of desire. As I cried, I moved my body against his and start to writhe underneath him. He stopped and looked at me and said "last chance Zavia. Do you know what you're doing?" "Yes" I whispered to him breathlessly "yes I do" and I reached up and caught his lips in mine initiating another kiss between us.

In that single moment, it was as if I had released him from some unseen bonds and with a fluid movement, he was positioned between my legs, kissing me and using his penis to rub insistently against my now wet lips. Sliding and pushing, not yet entering me but pressing against me as I moaned and squirmed anxiously. The anxiety overtook me and I reached between us to position him at my entrance. He tried to move my hands away, but I was insistent and with a guttural moan he plunged inside me. I felt a sharp pain like I was being torn apart but the intense searing pain was quickly replaced by a warm sense of pleasure that kept building as he stroked me insistently building up his rhythm and kissing and caressing me while stroking my insides intimately. I felt an intense pressure building inside me. Almost like what I imagined the inside of a pressure cooker must feel like. As the pressure built, I couldn't help but babble incoherently moaning his name "Nicholas, Nicholas, Nicholas" over and over again until I felt an explosion that caused me to shriek and stiffen my whole body, arching my back as he continued to stroke me.

As I was recovering from what I assumed was my first orgasm I felt his pace quicken and he pounded relentlessly into me. It felt painful and pleasurable all at the same time and I couldn't help but yelp each time he plunged back into me like a piston. I watched his face contort into an indescribable look that seemed like anguish and then he stiffened and let out a long sigh burying himself deeper inside me and becoming motionless and then heavy as his weight shifted. "Did you......?" "Yes, Zavia, I came". "Wow", I said. "Are you ok?" he asked kissing me tenderly on my shoulder and shifting his weight off me.

"Yes", I said, "I think I am". He shifted his body so he was lying next to me and pushed my hair out of my face. I smiled and said "that's the move that started all of this" and he chuckled. "Do you regret it?" he said, his face turning serious? "No. No I don't" I said, "it felt right and it still feels right". "Good", he said and kissed my forehead. As we lay there, he started to hum and hugged me to him, luckily it was a balmy night so I didn't feel cold even though I was lying buck naked next to him. It was strange how I felt so comfortable around him. There were no feelings of self-consciousness or nervousness I was happy just lying there with him. Too soon he said to me "Zavia I think we need to go back to the Sports Hall". "Yea we do," I said. "What's the time?" he turned his wrist and said "Shit, its 2 am. The party finishes at 2.30am so we have to get back there before the places empties out".

We both sat up and went to grab our clothes from the floor bumping our heads in unison. "Shit", I said as I rubbed my head and looked down. My inner thighs were smeared with blood and there was blood on the sofa. "Fuck, fuck, fuck," said Nicholas. "Ok, you need to get the towel and use it to wipe off your legs and I'll clean up in here," he said. I got up, grabbed the towel from earlier and scurried to the bathroom with my clothes. I cleaned up as best as I could thankful I wasn't wearing white underwear or the white dress that had been my second choice. Once my legs were clean, I smeared hand cream over my thighs, put on my underwear and then stepped into the dress. I raced back into the den where Nicholas already had on his pants and shirt although it was open and he was busy wiping the leather sofa. "Thankfully it's chocolate brown and leather," he said, "it should all look fine by tomorrow morning when Marguerite comes in. Have you got everything?" he asked me as he buttoned his shirt hurriedly and I said "yes. Can you zip me up, please?" "Sure" he replied and I turned my back to him. As we scanned the room to ensure, it looked as we had found it I smiled thinking I would honestly never forget this night. We bounded to the front door where I swapped my heels for flip flops and then we hurried back to the Sports Hall.

When we got there, people were slowly leaving although the sound system, still had ten minutes to play. I went into the hall ahead of Nicholas, who stopped to talk to some of the guys he knew. I made a beeline for Zee, who was sitting at a table with a bored looking guy who I didn't know very well. "Hey, Zee", I said. "Hey Zee? Where the fuck have you been?" she said. "I was worried about you!" "I was at Nicholas'" I said, "and we lost track of time" I said glad that the lights were still off so she couldn't see me flush. "Oh, you lost track of time huh? Ok. Whatever! Well Jorge here is our ride home" she said, "Jorge, we're ready". "Cool", he said finally perking up. As Zee and Jorge got up, Nicholas strolled in and I smiled. Zee coughed and I said nothing as he walked over to me and said "are you ok?" "Yes, I'm fine Nicholas, Zee and Jorge are going to take me home now". "Ok", he said "well call me tomorrow". "I will" I promised and he squeezed my hand before sauntering off.

For the whole drive home, Zee kept looking at me in the rear-view mirror and I kept avoiding her glances. I barely waited for the car to come to a halt outside my house before I opened the car door and hopped out saying "I'll call you tomorrow Zee" and skipping up the driveway. As I let myself in quietly and started towards the stairs, I saw the light flash on in the living room and my father appeared in the doorway. "Zavia, come in here for a minute please darling". I turned and frowned as I made my way towards the living room. "What's wrong Daddy?" I said feeling worried. "Nothing, I just wanted to talk to you". I silently walked into the living room and my father closed the door behind me. I guess he didn't want to disturb the rest of the house. He walked back over to his chair and sat down and said "take a seat. Do you want a drink?" "Rum and Coke would be nice" I said confidently and he smiled wryly and said "ok" while opening his drinks cupboard and pouring me a shot of rum and handing me a can of Coke with my glass. I opened the Coke and heard the satisfying fizzing and then poured half of it into my rum.

Once my drink was poured my father started talking to me "your Uncle Compton and I witnessed the exchange between you and Reece this evening and frankly I didn't like it. If you hadn't slapped him for calling you a whore, I would have and Uncle Compton was ready to murder him so we left once we knew Zee and Adam would look out for you and before we both ended up in jail". I looked at my father in surprise and dismay and said: "sorry you witnessed that Daddy". "No don't apologise Zavia, I just want to understand what you're thinking. Time and time again I have seen Reece make decisions for you and treat you like a possession. You're a bright girl Zavia and I had always expected you to be very successful at whatever you did. As a woman, I thought that one day you would want to get married and have a family but I didn't think that would be in the next few months. Remember there are three words I always ask you, children, to consider through all your life experiences. They are pride, dignity and character. I know that you possess these traits and I watched you display them ferociously this evening, but the questions I have for you is: Do you want a man who also shows these characteristics and do you think that Reece has them? I am not going to give you my opinion I just want you to think about that and ask yourself what kind of man disrespects his wife-to-be in such a public manner. Finish your drink and spend some time thinking about it and whatever conclusions you reach and decisions that they lead you to take will be fully supported by me." "Thank you, Daddy", I said feeling sober despite the rum burning a path down my throat. I got up, kissed my father goodnight and took my drink up to bed with me. "Make sure you wash the glass out before your mother starts on me for giving you rum" he called after me and I said "yes Daddy" as I walked up the stairs.

As I lay in bed reliving my evening, both the good and the bad I knew in my heart what the right decision was. This wasn't a choice between Nicholas and Reece it was a choice between the Rodrigues family name and tradition or me and I knew what my choice would be. I slept soundly that night, aided by the nightcap from my father. The next morning, as I opened my eyes and stretched, his words rang in my ears, pride, dignity and character and I resolved to deal with this situation today. I got out of bed and stuck my head out of my room to see if the bathroom was free. I needed to rinse the glass quickly before my mother did her rounds of checking on us kids. The coast seemed clear so I sprinted to the bathroom with the glass wrapped in my towel. I turned the shower on hoping to get a nice hot blast but instead the water was tepid. I quickly washed off the slight soreness between my legs reminding me of my night with Nicholas and bringing a flush to my cheeks. I went back into my room with my towel wrapped around me and was just pulling on a pair of shorts when my mother called up to me and said that Reece was here to see me. I took a deep breath and said "coming Mum. I pulled a t-shirt on and took a deep breath before going downstairs.

Reece was waiting for me outside on the front porch so I stepped outside and left the door slightly ajar so I wouldn't get locked out. "Do you want a drink, Reece?" I asked him. "No thanks," he said. I took a seat opposite him and looked at him expectantly. "Well", he said. "Do you want to apologise?" "I'm sorry I hit you," I said. "Is that it?" he asked angrily. "Yes. I don't think there's anything else that I need to be sorry for" I replied. "What?" He said arrogantly "aren't you sorry for embarrassing me and flaunting yourself with that Nicholas guy?" "I wasn't doing any of those things, so I don't need to apologise".

"Zavia, you can't be flaunting yourself with other men. It gives the impression that, that....", "That what?" I said, "I'm a whore?" He at least had the good grace to look a little embarrassed, but he still didn't apologise which was making me more resolute in my decision. "Well Zavia, it's not like I'm saying you were sleeping with him. I'm just saying think about how it looked". "Well maybe I did" I retorted cryptically. "Did what?" he said. But even as the question left his lips I could see comprehension dawning. "Did what Zavia?" he said more forcefully. I shrugged and looked at him feeling suddenly spiteful. "Did you sleep with him Zavia?" He said. I looked him dead in the eye and said "yes." And with that yes I released myself from the shackles that would have been a marriage into the Rodrigues family.

His green eyes met mine and I saw a flash of anger and pain in them and I immediately regretted the cruel way that I had broken the news to him. "My mother warned me about getting involved with you." He said, "you're a classless army brat and I've no idea why I thought I could turn a tramp into a lady." I jumped off my seat and rushed over to him screaming "get the fuck off my property you worthless, spineless mama's boy. If your mum is so perfect, why don't you marry her?" "You can't throw me out. Who do you think you are?" At this point the front door opened and my father loomed in the doorway his eyes glinting dangerously. "She is my daughter and she is telling you to leave so I suggest that you take your leave now young man". Reece looked at me and then my father and wordlessly walked towards his car that was parked outside our house.

I was shaking with anger and my father had to physically pull me back into the house as I was rooted to the spot. My mother was standing in the hall looking confused and Adam was standing at the bottom of the stairs with a glint in his eyes almost as dangerous as my father's. "I'm sure you guys will work it out," said my mother. "You know you, young people. Always arguing" she said hopefully, obviously seeing her dream wedding going up in flames. My father turned to her and said: "did you not hear what he said?" "I did," she said, "but we all say things that we regret in the heat of the moment". "Well, I don't regret anything," I said, "it's over between Reece and I and I won't be getting married". My mum looked visibly upset while Adam said "well I can drink to that" and my father nodded at me imperceptibly, a flash of understanding passing between us.

As we all stood there like statues the doorbell rang and my father said: "I swear if that boy is back I will kick his ass". "Make sure you leave a piece for me" Adam added and our father smiled wryly as he strode to the door and flung it open. There on the doorstep was Nicholas, "yes!" barked my father. "I hope you're not here on behalf of that Rodrigues boy." "Rodrigues boy?" said Nicholas confused. "No, he's our friend Dad. Nothing to do with Reece. Wassup Nicky said Adam explaining to our father while greeting Nicholas. "Come in." "Dad, this is Nicholas", I added. "Nicolette's son. My business partner for the placement". "Oh hello, young man. Apologies for the greeting but we've had a bit of trouble here this morning". "No problem sir. It's a pleasure to finally meet you. You weren't home when I was here last week". "Your father is Craven Roberts isn't he? I know him very well" said my father as he nodded approvingly and reached to shake Nicholas' hand. Obviously, his father was quite a significant man as my father added: "Give him my regards when you speak to him next please". "I will sir," said Nicholas. "I'll leave you guys to catch up now," my father said. "Your mother and I are going to the market, so you can go down to the family room".

I led Nicholas down the stairs to the family room where we sunk onto bean bags on the floor while I flicked the TV on. "So I guess Reece knows?" he said. "Yep," I said, "sorry I should have given you the heads up". "It's cool," he said "I'm glad he knows. I couldn't imagine having to creep around to see you". "Nicholas, don't get me wrong. I love what we did and I want to do it again, but I'm not sure I want to jump into a relationship with you right now". "I understand," he said. "I really like you and I love what we did last night but I'm not going to pressure you. The only thing I will say is that I don't want to share you. I'm willing to only be with you intimately if you can promise I won't have to share you". "I can promise that," I said, "I just don't want labels right now". "Cool", he said reaching over and pulling my beanbag closer to him so he could climb onto it which was completely impractical. "Get off my beanbag Roberts," I said and he laughed. "So on a serious note I'm going back to Berbice in a week," he said. "You know I'm going to miss you?" "Yea I will too," I said. It's been a full four weeks. We've seen each other every day". "Yes, I know but we both need to focus on our exams. Have you given any thought to where you are going to study?" He asked. "I'm thinking New York," I said. "Well, I'm not sure yet, still weighing up my options and I have to talk to my Dad as well". "Cool", I said. "You know I'm going to be home some weekends and it's only two months until the Summer break. We can chill together then". "Yep", I said feeling strangely calm.

Something was different with Nicholas. It was like having my best friend and a boyfriend relationship all rolled into one. I knew that whatever happened we would be ok and I would be ok. Nicholas and I spent the afternoon lazing around. My parents came back from the market and I was roped into helping to make Sunday dinner and Nicholas offered to help. He and Adam peeled potatoes and made a salad while mum and I did the hard work. The atmosphere in the kitchen was light-hearted and Dad even put on his Bob Marley – Exodus album on so we were all singing along in the kitchen.

Once dinner was ready, Adam went to put the potato peels in the rubbish bin and came back with a box that had my name on it. I opened it curiously and found a note from Mrs Rodrigues, Reece's mother with all the things I had left at Reece's over the past few months. The note said

"Dear Zavia

In light of the recent events and the demise of your relationship with my son, I thought it was best that you cut all contact with him. To assist in this healing process for him, I have enclosed all your belongings and ask that you return the engagement ring via the postal system.

Mrs Paul Rodrigues III."

I swear that woman was nuttier than a macadamia. I passed the note wordlessly to Adam, who read it out loud. My father was livid and grabbed the note from Adam "Well to fuck with them and her, Zavia. You aren't returning one shit. You can keep the ring as compensation for putting up with his bullshit" he exploded. "I don't know," I said "it feels weird. It's not like I'll even be wearing the ring anymore" I said as I absentmindedly twisted it around my finger. "You know what, give me the ring Zavia. I'll deal with this" said my father. I meekly pulled the ring off my finger and dropped it into my father's outstretched palm. "Right", he said. "Enough of them, let's go set up the table for dinner. Nicholas, I assume you're staying?" "Yes, Mr Fraser," said Nicholas.

As we ferried serving spoons, cutlery, and dishes between the kitchen and the dining room, Nicholas pulled me aside and said "Your dad is great. I really like him". "Thanks", I said "he does come through for us in a crisis, guess it's all the military training". "Are you ok though Zav? Nicholas probed, "it can't be easy for you". "It is hard," I said, "I miss Reece a little bit and I feel kinda sad but I know I'm making the right decision and I have to be firm in my conviction". "That's my girl," he said, tenderly stroking my face. At that precise moment, JoJo and Lucky came running through the hall and we jumped back creating a space between us. Dinner was uneventful. Nicholas, Adam and my dad talked about sports and JoJo kept looking at Nicholas shyly and smiling. My mother remarked on Nicholas' manners after the meal when he had gone home and she was suitably impressed with him being Nicolette's son. So all in all a great end to what could have been a bad day.

NICHOLAS

A week later Nicholas was back at school and I was immersed in exam preparation and coursework. We spoke on the telephone each night and we planned to meet up when he was back the following weekend for the Labour Day holiday. I couldn't wait for him to be back so we could make love again. After my first time, we hadn't repeated it and I was curious to see how it would feel again.

The Labour Day weekend was a chance to let my hair down from studying and let off some steam. Nicholas would be back from the Friday night and we had agreed that we would spend most of the weekend together. First, he would be attending my family barbeque on Saturday and then on Sunday, Nicolette had an annual beach party that I was invited to. We would be staying at her beach house returning sometime on Tuesday to avoid the bank holiday traffic. Nicholas would go back to school from there and Nicolette would bring me home.

On Friday evening, I was stuck in the kitchen helping to prepare meat for the barbeque. Our house was heaving with people. All of my siblings were back for the barbeque as it was also a birthday celebration for Lucky and my father. Zee was also helping out with the preparation and there was a warm camaraderie in the kitchen. All the girls were helping our mother and because we were quite a traditional family the boys were helping our father in the yard. Zee and I were chopping cabbages ready for coleslaw and Lola was helping us. Audrey and Vanessa, my second eldest sister, were tidying up the dining room and living room ready for when the house would be filled with guests.

As I was mixing the coleslaw the doorbell rang and Audrey called "I'll get it", a couple of minutes later, Audrey walked into the room saying "a cute guy is asking for you Zavia. Says his name is Nicholas". I sprung up from the table while Lola raised her eyebrows quizzically at Zee, she had been travelling with Tyrone for months so I hadn't told her about Nicholas yet. When I got to the door, Nicholas was standing there waiting. As he saw me, his face broke into a smile and my heart leapt, I hadn't even appreciated how much I missed him. "Hey you," he said, poking me in the side. "Hey yourself," I said giving him a playful punch on the arm. "It's been awhile." "I know," he said. "Wish I could hug you and kiss you" he whispered. "Me too, but I'm sure at least two of my sisters are peeping at us and the boys are all over the yard so one could pop up at any minute, so we will just have to wait," I said despondently. "Well, we have the whole night on Sunday night and Monday night," he said. "You did ask your parents right?" "Yes", I said "and it's fine, as long as I'm back by 3pm on Tuesday, they are cool with it. I think they're kind of waiting for me to break down about the engagement so anything they can see distracting me they welcome it". "Perfect," he said. "I have no problem being a distraction for you". I was looking around expectantly and Nicholas said: "What are you waiting for?" "I was just thinking that it has been a whole five minutes without one of my siblings interrupting us. That's a minor miracle".

I apparently spoke too soon because there was suddenly an almighty crash and Nicholas and I went running down the front steps and around to the side of the house. There Adam stood on a ladder while Ravin, my eldest brother and Aidan looked at some beams on the floor. "What happened?" I said, "Ravin dropped a pole as he was passing it to me. He's such a pretty boy. Too good for yard work". Ravin kissed his teeth and said "Shut up! Just because I'm not a Neanderthal like you". As Adam turned to reply, he noticed Nicholas and said: "Yo Nicky, when did you get back?" "Bout half hour ago," said Nicholas. "Cool! You busy?" Said Adam. "Nah, going to shoot hoops in about an hour but till then I'm free" Nicholas replied. "Great," said Adam "Grab a beam. Ravin, Aidan, this is Nicky, one of the basketball stars of the future and Zavia's latest love interest". "Oh shut up Adam," I said. "I'm going back to the kitchen. See you later Nicholas". "Cool, I'll call out for you before I leave Zav," he said without looking at me as Aidan and Ravin eyed him curiously. I made my way around to the back of the house and went up the stairs to the kitchen's back door. No sooner as I stepped foot back in the kitchen, Lola was already on my case saying "he's cute Zavia". "Yes, he is," I said. "Nice physique and those eyes! What's that about?" Said Vanessa, who was doing dishes. "Who is he?" she added. "We worked together on a project and became friends" I replied. Zee coughed violently and I walked over to her and slapped her hard on the back saying "let me help you with that Zee" and she pushed me away laughing. "Well, girl if you don't wanna upgrade him out of the friend box then I will," said Audrey. At only three years older than me we had the closest thing to sibling rivalry in the family and it could on occasion cause friction. "Leave him alone Auds," I said. "Oh, so you are planning an upgrade. Cool", she said "I know to keep my mitts off. "Whatever," I said.

We worked solidly in the kitchen for the next three hours with the only interruption being when Nicholas popped his head around to let me know that he was leaving. I wiped my hands on my apron conscious that I stunk of onions and walked him to the front door. We stole a quick kiss in the hallway as he whispered to me "I'm looking forward to this weekend babe." "Me too," I said. "Ok! Gotta go" he said as he bounded down the stairs and jumped into Nicolette's jeep that he was driving that day.

After a gruelling night in the kitchen I needed a long nights sleep but alas at 6am, the following morning my father brought out his old claxon and got us all up. Vanessa had stayed at a hotel with her husband Stephen and their twin baby sons while Ravin had stayed with Lola and Tyrone while the rest of us were all home. *Lucky them* I thought betting that they would be shopping and doing their hair before they came anywhere near the house to help. I couldn't wait to leave for university so I could avoid these prep sessions before big events.

I got out of bed rubbing my eyes and heard Audrey groaning, she was in the bed on the other side of the room and she said: "Jeez I forgot how annoying that sound is". "Tell me about it," I said. We pulled on leggings and t-shirts and walked into our parents' room with our toothbrushes. We knew it would be almost impossible to get into the other bathroom so we took turns to brush our teeth and do our hair in Mum's bathroom being sure to dry the sink so she didn't know. We knew she suspected we used her bathroom, but we always left it tidy so there was no proof.

After a solid four hours of work, it was time to get the family ready for the event, which started at midday. Audrey and I volunteered to get Lucky and JoJo ready and we had a great time choosing matching outfits for them and Audrey took charge of styling all our hair. It was at times like this that I missed having Audrey around, but I knew that wistfulness would be short-lived.

By about 1pm the barbeque was in full swing. Most of our parents' guests had arrived and the chicken was sizzling and creating a delicious aroma in the air. Adam and Aidan were taking turns to manage the sound system, everyone had a charged glass and I looked around thinking I have a beautiful family and a beautiful life. The sun beat down on my face and I felt the warmth of its rays as well as the warm feeling of being in the bosom of a large, rambunctious family.

The icing on the cake was when Nicholas arrived. He had brought Nicolette with him and he moved effortlessly between the adult crowd and the youngsters seemingly at ease with both. Nicolette was charming as usual. I marvelled at her ability to make women like her even though she was a beautiful, young and sexy woman who was single and notorious for having a child with a married man which usually worried the Georgetown society wives.

The evening was spent eating, playing rounders and listening to the heavy beats of the sound system as Adam took to the decks and pumped out some fast soca music getting everyone on their feet. I remember thinking that I would hold this night in my memory as a happy time for me, my brothers and sisters.

The next morning, I was exempt from clean-up duty as I was getting ready to go to the Summer House with Nicholas and Nicolette. I spent almost an hour agonising over what to wear and then with only half an hour to spare, Audrey made the decision for me by accidentally spilling coffee on one of my outfits. I ended up wearing a navy and white sailor suit which Lola had bought on one of her many trips. "That looks much better than those shorts that you were going to wear," said Audrey. "Yea, you would say that" I snarled still angry that I was an outfit down because of her.

As I was packing my toiletries, I heard the phone ringing down the hall. I wondered who would pick it up hoping that it wouldn't be Aidan as he could sometimes be a little over protective of me. As I heard someone striding towards my room, chattering away I was glad when my ears recognised Adam's voice and I opened the door to look at him. "Oh here she is now," he said, "I didn't know that you two were going on a cruise," he said chuckling while I grabbed the phone away from him. "Hi," I said into the phone. "Hey baby, it's me" I heard Nicholas reply. "I'm leaving to come get you in about five minutes. So be ready" he said. "Perfect! I'm almost ready" I said while Audrey critically surveyed the pile of items strewn on the bed and floor in the room next to my weekend bag.

I scowled at her, the annoyance about my outfit rising again and as I clicked off from Nicholas I started to pick up things and stuff them either into my bag or back into the wardrobe. "Do you think you have enough stuff in there?" Audrey said, "I mean you are going for two whole nights after all! Of course, you need six pairs of underwear". "I'm just being prepared" I snorted. "Yea prepared for what, though?" she replied, "you're such a dumbass sometimes Zavia". "You'd know wouldn't you Auds, after all, it takes one to know one," I said sarcastically. Just as she was about to answer me, we heard a car horn tooting and I grabbed my bag and ran downstairs. My mother and father were in the kitchen so I rushed in to say goodbye to them before I went out to Nicolette's jeep. My father strolled behind me and called out to Nicholas, "Take care of my baby please young man" and Nicholas saluted him and said, "yes sir!" As I slid into the jeep, I smiled at Nicholas watching how the sun glinted on his sunshades and thinking about how much I was looking forward to making love to him again.

Once we got to Nicolette's, he told me to wait in the jeep while he went to tell Nicolette that we were ready to go. I slipped into the back seat positioning myself under the sunroof so that I could take advantage of the hot sun beating down on me. With my eyes closed, I lay back on the seat listening to the bustle as Nicolette and Nicholas made their way to the car. Nicolette was complaining because Nicholas had three bags. As I heard her say three bags, I opened my eyes and peeked out. Nicholas had a large holdall, a backpack and a wheeled trolley. "You're kidding right?" I said. "Nope Zavia it appears that he is serious," Nicolette said with a mock scowl. "What's with all the bags?" "It's sports stuff" he replied, "I've got snorkelling gear, cricket stuff, tennis racquets and my swimming stuff". Nicolette rolled her eyes and I said "Jeez Nicholas we're only going for a couple of days and I definitely don't expect to be exerting myself too much" I said looking at him meaningfully. He looked back at me his eyes suddenly flickering with understanding and he dropped the holdall on the floor and said "Let me take all this crap back. All I kinda need is clothes". "Good plan," I told him smiling mischievously. Nicolette looked from me to Nicholas in confusion, shook her head and said "Great! Glad Zavia has made you finally see sense."

It took us two hours to drive to Nicolette's Summerhouse in Berbice. It was just near to the beach and it was a sprawling property with ten bedrooms and lots of land. In the driveway there were already other vehicles parked and there was a buzz of activity emanating from the house and I saw some guys preparing a barbeque drum. "Time to party," said Nicholas jumping out of the jeep before Nicolette had even properly brought it to a halt. "For God's sake, Nicky can you calm down?" Nicolette yelled at him. He laughed and said "chill and stop being such a mum" "I am your mum" Nicolette protested but even she smiled as she said it. I got out of the jeep more slowly than Nicholas and waited for Nicolette as Nicholas had already walked ahead. Suddenly I felt slightly overwhelmed by spending the weekend here with lots of strangers. Nicolette almost sensed this and said "Don't worry my friends and family are easy-going and you won't be the only newbie. Only thing is, you're the first girl that Nicky has invited so expect to be grilled by his aunts". *Oh great*, I thought. And as if on cue a girl who looked a couple of years older than me opened the door and came wandering out saying "Hi Aunty Nic" "Hey Riri. How you doing?" "I'm cool Aunty, glad for the break. I'm so busy with University that this is a welcome pause from my exams." "Good! I'm pleased that you're getting a break honey. I'm looking forward to a proper catch up with you. Oh my, where are my manners?" Nicolette added as she turned towards me. "This is Zavia, Nicky's friend". "Sup Zavia, nice to meet Nicky's first official girlfriend," she said. I stammered and said, "hhhhhi nice to meet you". "You're not his usual type," she said. "He usually goes for really glamorous looking girls, and airheads but Aunt Nic tells me that you are smart and you're obviously pretty. What are you planning on studying at University?" "I'm still making up my mind". I replied hesitantly, taken aback by her candour. "I like all aspects of business studies so I'm struggling to make a final decision" "Ok that's cool," she said. "I'm doing psychology which is so interesting. I find humans and their norms and habits are fascinating." I looked at the enthralled expression on her face and vowed that I would find something to study that made me feel as passionate as she seemed to be.

I soon learned that RiRi was just one of Nicholas' female cousins. He came from a family full of girls and the generations were all skewed because Nicolette had given birth to him at 17. His youngest aunt was also a year older than us, like RiRi, and her name was Matilda or Mattie as the family called her. Mattie arrived about an hour after us. She lived in Berbice so was just over to hang out and as her car turned onto the street, we could hear it approach as it blared reggae music. I looked up curiously from the chair I was sitting in on the verandah and was surprised to see a light skinned girl with a head full of blonde-streaked curls step out of a red sports car. She was wearing a bikini top with denim cut off shorts and she strode in with an air of confidence that I could only wish for. "Hey, Mattie" drawled Lester,

Nicholas' uncle who was setting up the barbeque in the yard. "Hey bro" she replied smiling a megawatt smile. "Where's Mum?" she said, "She isn't at home". "She's just at Aunt Lucy's" he replied "she'll be here later. Aunt Lucy needed a lift. "Ok great. So who's here?" she asked. "Nicky, his girl, Nic, Riri and Brian's lot". "Ok," she said "and where's Brian?" "He's at the back picking coconuts and fruit to make drink". "Cool," she said, "let me go and check out this girl Nicky's brought up here. I hope it ain't one of the usual hoes that he hangs with". "Ahem, the potential hoe is on the verandah above your head so you might want to lower your voice". We didn't hear anything more from Mattie, but we heard Lester chuckling and a couple of minutes later the front door opened and we heard someone moving around the house.

After a while, Mattie appeared at the verandah door and said "Hey whassup" she was looking in our general direction so I said "hi." Nicholas turned to look at her and said "oh now you wanna be all polite? You shoulda tried that before you came in the yard talking trash" he said. "Who was talking trash? I was stating a fact. You're always hanging with hoes. Your mum and my mum don't even know that you always seem to pick the sluttiest gyals to hang out with and as your aunt it's my responsibility to make sure you don't bring one of them tricks to the family barbeque." She said sanctimoniously. "My aunt? Are you fucking kidding me? You're barely a year older than me" "14 months actually!" she replied snootily. "Oh fuck off Mattie! The point is that Zavia is not a hoe." He said forcefully. "Well I'll be the judge of that" she retorted. Neither of them intending to back down. At this point, I was thankful when RiRi strode onto the verandah and said "Would you two fuckwits shut up! Mattie learn to keep your mouth shut or whisper and Nicky let's keep the drama to a minimum, please. Zavia is a bright girl headed for University and she comes from a good family. I'm fairly sure she doesn't sleep around and even if she is a hoe, Nicky is a big boy he has to learn how to handle his women" Nicholas nodded and jutted out his chin defiantly and Mattie looked at Riri with the same defiant stare.

I was vaguely amused because Nicky and Mattie looked very similar despite their different colouring and they were obviously as stubborn as each other. "Anyhow," I said, getting up "why don't we go for a walk. You can show me around the grounds, Nicky", I said using his nickname as a way to calm him down. He looked at me and said "what are you buttering me up for? You never call me Nicky!" I laughed and said, "you'll see". He grabbed me around my waist and we walked down the stairs into the backyard. Beyond the fence, there were lots of fruit trees and Nicholas opened a gate and we slipped through. It felt so free to be here walking with Nicholas. It was weird, I couldn't remember ever feeling this free with Reece. Somehow it always felt like I was holding my breath, waiting to exhale. Yet here, with Nicholas, I was taking in gulps of fresh air and it felt great. Nicholas and I had a relaxing couple of days. We made love repeatedly, sneaking away during the afternoon before the barbeque as well as numerous times during the night because Nicolette was much more relaxed about things like our sleeping arrangements.

The weeks after the Labour Day weekend seemed to go by in a rush. I was holed up in my room, studying most of the time and I hardly spoke to Nicholas because phone time at his school was reduced during exams. I remember the last day of exams. Adam and I both had a maths exam and for the last hour, it felt like I was itching to jump out of my own skin. When the alarm went, to mark the end of the exam, I felt faint with relief and rolled down my face. A few people looked at me as I bawled at my desk waiting to be let out and I saw Adam cutting his eyes at me as I was no doubt embarrassing him. When we were finally let out, I watched as the boys whooped and pummelled each other and I went looking for Zee. I found her in our usual spot under a gigantic tree in the school yard. We embraced each other with relief and she smiled and said "Welcome to the rest of your life Ms Fraser" and I laughed.

When I got home that afternoon, there was a message scrawled on a piece of paper in my room saying that Nicholas had called and would call back at 8pm. I smiled and looked at my watch already counting down the time until I spoke to him. It felt weird sitting on my bed without having to worry about studying or thinking about all the other school related stuff that I should be doing. I planned to enjoy my time off because my father had already arranged for both Adam and me to do work experience during the Summer so the relaxation was going to be short-lived. Adam had got a job at the Sports Hall as a lifeguard and I would be working with my cousin Nevlyn, who was the Human Resources Director at Josiah King, a prominent law and accountancy firm. I was looking forward to being immersed in the corporate world.

As I lay there thinking about what I would wear to work, I heard the telephone ringing. I didn't even move, I really couldn't be bothered until I heard my mother's voice shouting "Zavia it's for you, pick up". I went into the hallway and picked up the phone that was on the table next to the bathroom and shouted: "Got it, Mum." It was Nicholas "Hey sweetness," he said. "Hey yourself" I replied, smiling from ear to ear. "So," he said, "I've got some bad news". "Uh huh", I said as an icy cold grip took hold of my heart. "What's up?" I said hoping that my voice didn't betray the quickening of my heartbeat. "I don't think I can continue to chill with you the way we've been chilling". "Ok, that's cool," I said breezily trying to hurry the conversation along so I could go to my room and cry. I didn't even notice when I fell for Nicholas, but obviously, I had or it wouldn't hurt so much hearing him say that we couldn't chill together anymore. "Anyhow, I gotta go," I said not even hearing what he had been saying. "Zavia, I know you couldn't have heard me so let me repeat it and I want you to listen". "Ok", I whispered wondering why he wanted to humiliate and upset me by repeating his rejection speech. "I can't chill with you the way we have been because I really like you and I want you to be my girlfriend officially. I want to take you places on my arm and show everyone that you're my girl. Are you down for that?" My heart leapt with joy and I giggled and said: "yeah I think I can be down with that". "Good," he said, "Cos I'm coming home in two days and it's RiRi's birthday so there's a big party for her and I want you to be my date. It's at Night Flight so be ready to dazzle. "Can Zee come too?" I said "yea she can though I think that Craig was planning on asking her anyway. He knows RiRi and he mentioned Zee's name to me when we were talking about dates". "Cool," I said. "I can't wait". "Well, I can't wait for either, I've missed you." "Me too" I replied. "Well, anyhow," he said, "I gotta go, but I wanted to give my girl a call". I smiled and said, "cool, talk to you tomorrow baby".

The next two days were filled with plans of what to wear and how to do my hair. As usual, Zee and I were always changing our outfits and it felt so great to be worrying about something other than exams. On Friday, Nicholas picked me up. I had told my parents that I would be out all night as Nicolette was doing breakfast at her house after the party that was sure to last into the early hours of the morning. Surprisingly my mother had no objections but I think that was due in part to my father's influence as well as the fact that I had finished my exams.

The night was perfect and so was the rest of our summer. We

91

spent two idyllic months together. Between work experience and relaxing with Nicholas I couldn't have asked for a better two months. There was a natural chemistry between us that required no effort and Nicholas was very good at giving me space so I never felt claustrophobic the way that I had with Reece. It was a bittersweet relationship because we had agreed that we would break up at the end of Summer because we both felt we were too young to settle down and have a long distance relationship. But in our hearts, we also knew that if we had been staying in the same country, we wouldn't have been ready to end things just yet. But alas Nicholas was going to Toronto to attend University on a sports scholarship and I would be going to the University of Florida.

Soon it was time for us to say goodbye. Nicholas had to leave two weeks before me so we spent his last evening hanging out at Nicolette's house listening to music and pretending it wasn't our last night together. "Are you gonna write to me?" I said. "Yes Zav, I'll write to you and when I can, I'll call you too." "Good," I said leaning over to hug him tightly feeling tears pricking at the back of my eyes. We sat like that in an awkward hugging position for what seemed like ages until Nicolette pushed open the door to the study and told us to go to bed as it was late. I slept at their house that night and Nicolette took me home on the way to the airport. I waved goodbye to Nicholas and stood to watch Nicolette's Jeep until it was just a speck in the distance.

KIERON

When I got to University, my schedule was hectic. Nicholas and I tried to keep in touch, but we seemed to often miss each other and after a few weeks, we both stopped trying. I was attending a prestigious all-female University and I approached University life with the same gusto as I had applied to my high school days. My Bachelor's Degree years went by in a flash. I lived in dorms and I loved the hustle and bustle of being in a house even busier than my home. Once I decided to stay on to do my Masters I knew that I needed more peace so I moved into an off-campus apartment. My roommate, assigned by the college, was Leila, a stunning but introverted Bajan girl. Almost the complete opposite of me. We were different but hit it off from the beginning so things were cool.

Although Leila was quieter than me, we often went out to town for a drink or just to hang out. She was the perfect roommate, never too loud and not a distraction. She was very different to the girls I was usually friends with, but somehow it worked. We enjoyed living together but we never really developed a strong friendship. Zee was still my best friend and we emailed each other regularly and sometimes called as she was in Jamaica studying nutrition and fashion. Trust Zee to do a weird combination.

As we got to the end of our first Master's year, I couldn't believe how time had flown. We had to reapply for housing and Leila and I decided to reapply to continue being roommates. We studied different subjects and had different friends so it meant that our apartment became a safe and calm haven for both of us. Despite our different social circles, Leila and I still went out occasionally. One evening, we were sitting at a comedy night listening to some absolutely awful wannabe comedians doing their routines when a gorgeous guy slipped into the booth next to Leila and started to flirt with her. I took my cue to leave and went to the bar to chill out with some people I knew from our building.

Later, Leila signalled that she was ready to go home and we left. In the taxi, I grilled her about the guy and found out his name was Kieron and he had asked her out on a date. She shyly told me that she couldn't believe he was interested in her because he was a basketball player on the college team and he was also one of the most popular sportsmen on campus. I was always surprised that she didn't know how stunning she was so I reminded her.

A few weeks later I came home to find Leila crying in her room saying that Kieron seemed too busy for her and she was afraid that he was cheating on her. I tried to calm her down, but she wouldn't stop crying. Suddenly she sat up in bed sniffing and said "I know. Why don't you call him and pretend to be interested in him and see if he is willing to meet you?" I wasn't convinced that it would work but once she had focused on this as an answer, I found it hard to tell her no. We agreed that I would call him that weekend when I was away on a netball team retreat so that our apartment number was not on his caller id. On Friday night, I left for the retreat armed with the number and told Leila to call me on Sunday morning to discuss what had happened.

On Saturday, I couldn't get through to Kieron but on Sunday morning I tried one more time and he answered. When I heard his voice over the phone, I was shocked at the jolt that I felt. His voice was deep and sexy like liquid chocolate, I quickly introduced myself as Jade and explained that I had seen him around campus and wanted to get to know him better. At first, he was a little reticent about sharing information because he wanted to know who I was and how I got his number but I readily supplied all the right answers and he relaxed. After a few moments, I slipped into my own personality and we talked about everything including our favourite basketball team, the Chicago Bulls. We also shared an interest in Greek Mythology and a love of hot dogs and onions with lots of ketchup. I looked at my watch and saw that we had talked for almost three hours. It was as if we had known each other for years. The real purpose of the call was forgotten as I became more and more engrossed in Kieron.

As I was talking, I looked at my cell phone and saw a text message from Leila

94

"Well? what happened with Kieron."

and I was jolted back to reality, "Oh I have to go" I said. "Why don't we meet up? He replied and I found myself agreeing that it would be great to meet up for a coffee sometime in our favourite bookstore. He asked for my number so we could confirm arrangements for the next week Saturday, but I told him I would send him a message once I had a confirmed time in mind and we clicked off. Immediately, the phone rang again. It was Leila asking who on earth I had been talking to all morning and asking what had happened with Kieron. I don't know why but I didn't have the heart to tell her that I had been talking to him, somehow it felt disloyal and I just couldn't reconcile the Kieron I had spoken to with the distant guy that she had described.

A few of hours later I was getting ready to go to back to University when my phone beeped. I looked down at the display and noticed a text message from a number that I didn't recognise. The message was from Kieron.

"Zavia if you wanted to get to know me better you could have said, I must say that you're alter ego Jade is intriguing and I definitely want to get to know her."

I know I should have just ignored the message and left Leila to deal with her own drama but I was so drawn in by Kieron that I replied to ask him how he got my number. I justified this decision by telling myself I was only tying up loose ends, but honestly, I knew that I wanted our banter to continue for as long as possible. Since coming to University, I hadn't clicked with anyone, the way I'd clicked with Kieron. It was just my luck that he was my roommate's on/off boyfriend.

His response clicked through to my phone in seconds

" I recognised your voice almost immediately, I remembered it from the night when Leila and I met, it was so distinctive. So I looked you up in the college directory. Are we meeting at the Bookstore next Saturday?"

I chuckled at his audacity finding it an affront and an aphrodisiac all at the same time. I found myself compelled to confirm my meeting with him although I changed the venue to the out of town bookstore. When I got home, Leila was still trying to convince me to call Kieron so that I could get information from him. I fobbed her off suggesting that she should probably talk to Kieron if she were worried about the state of their relationship.

On Saturday morning, I awoke bright and early still smiling at the text message exchange Kieron and I had enjoyed the previous night talking about the alignment of stars and swapping details about all our likes and dislikes. We had spent the last few days texting each other. I quickly rushed through my chores and carefully chose an outfit that I was sure would knock him dead before I started to tame my unruly mane of hair. I slicked my hair back into a ponytail with some wisps falling on my face, grabbed a pile of books and told Leila that I was going to study for the day. I got into my car and went to meet Kieron at the out of town bookstore. When I got there, I noticed there was an open mike session for budding poets. I sat at a table near the back to wait for him while I listened to the performers. Suddenly I heard that familiar gravelly voice and saw Kieron standing to recite a poem

"She walked into the room with her mane of hair,

Like a lioness, without a care,

Lips like berries and the colour of cherries,

waiting for someone to make her day

someone to love her and make it okay!

Heartbreak is written all over her face

As she sits here, in this lonely place

Her face tells a story of lies she's been told

Etched with the pain of being left in the cold

I wonder sweet lady

Would you give me a try?

I promise that I won't make you cry."

As he ended his poem, I felt myself mesmerised, imagining that we were alone in the room and that no one else existed. He exited the stage to rapturous applause and found myself clapping with the rest of the enamoured audience. As he made his way towards my table, purposefully, my heart rate quickened and I knew that I was in trouble emotionally more than I had been willing to admit, even to myself.

That afternoon, we listened and critiqued other poets and looked at books. He bought me a beautifully bound version of the Song of Solomon, taken from the Bible. He told me that it was the greatest love story ever told. As we walked to my car, hands entwined I wished that we had met under different circumstances. I felt sorry for Leila, but I genuinely believed that Kieron might be the one. I was so caught up in the moment that my guilt was fleeting. As I tried to open my car door, he kissed my neck and as I turned to tell him to stop my lips found his. It was like being in a different world, where time stood still. His kiss made me feel warm as if I was on a beach under the setting sun instead of a chilly car park in January. I was the first one to break the kiss as I told him "I have to go. Leila will be wondering where I am." That effectively broke the spell and I got into my car thinking it had been the best afternoon of my life, but now we had to return to reality. It had just been a snippet of what might have been, but now we would both have to avoid each other so Leila didn't get hurt.

When I got home, I went to my room and checked my emails. There was a message from Kieron explaining what a great time he'd had and begging me not to let today be the last day. I wondered what to do, torn between how it would look if I took away my roommate's boyfriend and my growing feelings for Kieron. Realistically, I knew that I would see him again. I was never one for the "sisterhood". I believed in equal rights for women, but I sure as hell didn't feel a kinship with everyone who had a vagina and a pair of breasts. It took more than that to gain my loyalty and I guess Leila hadn't done enough.

A couple of months later and Kieron and I were still together. After that magical day in the bookshop, we pretty much stole every moment that we could to be together. I admit I felt guilty as I heard Leila try to rationalise why he was no longer interested in dating her, but I couldn't help myself. He was like a drug. As he lived off campus, I spent more and more time at his apartment just relaxing, studying and enjoying the little cocoon that we had created. Leila noticed that I wasn't home very much and asked me about this mystery man. I laughed and said I didn't know what she was talking about. A week later, on my 20th birthday, Kieron sent me twenty red roses and Leila raised the question of the mystery boyfriend again. I quickly fabricated a pretend boyfriend Solomon to help me manage her questions about my absence and I basked in the knowledge that Kieron loved me, hoping that it would be enough to assuage the feelings of guilt.

As we approached our final exams, Kieron had to go on a trip which meant I was at the apartment more than usual. I went to knock on Leila's door and bounded in, without waiting for her to answer, as I usually did. I was horrified to see her hurriedly pulling on a cardigan which hid a multitude of cuts on her arm. I was speechless; I looked at her as she studiously ignored my gaze and acted like nothing was wrong. She asked me what I needed, but I couldn't say anything. I was so stunned. Finally, I blurted out "What are those marks on your arm?" and moved closer to her to see better. As I reached for her arm, she flinched and pulled away eyes flashing in pain and anger. "Leave me alone. I'm fine" she said. "But how can I Leila? Did you do that to yourself?" She looked at me with tears glistening in her eyes and nodded affirmation. "But why?" I asked. She shrugged her shoulders and said it wasn't important but at that moment it was the most important thing that I could contemplate. I guided her to her bed and sat next to her, "I'm listening" I said encouragingly. And then she poured out all the hurt and confusion that she had felt when Kieron had stopped returning her calls. She explained how much she had loved him and although it made no sense, he was everything she had ever wanted. She also explained exactly how he had broken it off with her. I never knew the details and in my hazy, loved- up state I had never bothered to make sure that he had done it in a way to leave Leila's self-respect, esteem and value intact. I had fooled myself that it wasn't my business but by stealing him I had made it my business!

She explained that they had bought advance tickets to see their favourite rapper T-Bone. On the day of the concert, she had tried to get hold of him to confirm arrangements. When he had finally returned her calls an hour before the show, he told her to drive there as he was caught up and would meet her there. She got ready taking her time to choose the "perfect" outfit and left for the concert. When she got there, she tried his cell again but there was a weak signal at the venue so she went in to wait knowing that he had his own ticket so could meet her at the exclusive booth she had bought for them. She explained that there had been a full moon and she could see it through the skylight in the booth. As I listened, my heart sank as I knew what was coming next. I remembered that night vividly. I had been having second thoughts about Kieron and I and had tried to finish it. He didn't want it to end so he convinced me to stay and talk. We had sat on his balcony talking all night making plans for the future while we looked at the full shimmery moon. I couldn't believe that he had left her there that night, dateless and alone without so much as a call. I understood that he was trying not to hurt me by ignoring her calls and texts but I wouldn't have wished that experience on my worst enemy much less someone who I considered a friend. I felt like throwing up, the guilt was like a stab to my heart!

As I listened to Leila, explain how worthless she felt while waiting I couldn't feel more bad about myself. She explained that she had tried to think of good reasons why he hadn't shown up. She had checked her phone repeatedly and tried to call him, almost hoping that he was dead or seriously injured so that she could justify being left there like a piece of dirt. While she recounted the tale, she absentmindedly rubbed her scars and cried. I was struck by how selfish I had been and about how every action has a consequence whether intended or not. I had destroyed one of the sweetest people I knew because of my own lack of self-control.

She was still talking as she explained that she now knew that Kieron had been seeing someone else. One of his friends' girlfriends had told her that he was all loved up now and they hardly saw him. She was saying that she wanted to meet the other girl so that she could understand what she was lacking. I quickly told her that it wasn't a comparison and that I was sure the other girl wasn't worth it. Maybe I was too vehement because she looked at me a little strangely. After telling me the story, she seemed more composed. I excused myself and sent Kieron a message saying that when he was back, we needed to talk. As I went to throw my phone on the bed, I suddenly felt extremely light headed and had to slump against the door frame until the feeling passed. That evening I bought a bottle of wine to cheer up Leila and I. We watched soppy movies and drank wine and ate chocolate. The next morning, I felt so sick and hungover, I threw up all day and felt generally rough. The next few days I still felt lethargic, but all my energy was taken up trying to lift Leila's spirits so I didn't have time to focus on being ill.

A week later I was rushing to class when I bumped into one of the first-years. I heard someone saying my name and felt a sharp pain in the back of my head. As I slowly opened my eyes, I found myself staring into the eyes of the resident first-aider. She explained that I had briefly lost consciousness. They weren't sure if I had fainted or been knocked unconscious so she wanted me to take my time getting up. As I sat up, she asked me whether I was stressed out and whether I had eaten. I admitted that I had been partying hard while also trying to keep up with coursework and study. She advised me to take it easy and cut back on the drinking and then sent me on my way.

That evening I was idly updating my diary when I noticed that my period was late. Then it hit me like a thunderbolt, I hadn't had a period for over 6 weeks. But I couldn't be, could I? My head started to spin and I tried frantically to rationalise that stress sometimes messes up my cycle but in my heart of hearts I knew that I was pregnant with Kieron's baby. How could everything have got so messed up? I had been waiting for him to come back so that I could break up with him because

I couldn't stand the pain that I had caused Leila and now I was going to have to tell him that I was pregnant. What a MESS! He was due back in a couple of days and I decided to put it out of my mind and pretend that it wasn't happening. Pretend that my life wasn't in tatters. So as I counted down to Kieron coming home, I threw myself into studying and chilling with Leila. If she noticed that I was preoccupied, she didn't mention it and we never spoke of why she was wearing long sleeves during an unusually hot period in May.

Finally, it was the day that Kieron was due back. His flight would land in the afternoon and I had arranged to meet him at our bookstore. I got up to take a shower and prepare for a Zumba class when I was crippled by a cramp. It felt like a period cramp but much more severe. The pain took my breath away and I struggled to stand straight. As the pain subsided, I was walking to the bathroom when I felt a warm rush between my legs. I looked down, horrified to see blood running down my thighs. Despite not wanting to be pregnant the rush of anxiety that gripped me was like nothing I had ever felt. I cried and muttered prayers begging God to save my baby. As I stood there rooted to the spot watching the crimson pool of my blood grow around my feet Leila opened her door and gasped. "What's wrong Zavia?" she asked. I couldn't answer I just stood there with tears silently trickling down my face. She asked me if I was in pain and I nodded. She came to hold my hand and I squeezed it as another cramp ripped through me. I whispered that I needed a doctor but begged her not to leave me. She reached into my dressing gown for my cell phone and dialled for an ambulance. I was still standing there with her when they arrived. They took me to the hospital and she came with me as I silently cried. Once there, they examined me and found that two of my eggs had been fertilised. One had travelled into my fallopian tube causing an ectopic pregnancy and the other was also being expelled due to the stress on my body. They took me into surgery to remove both as the risk was too great to let nature take its course. I couldn't do anything but numbly consent to surgery and then they knocked me out.

When I woke up the next morning, Kieron was sitting on the bed staring at me, holding my hand. His face was streaked with tears and he looked so tired, but I couldn't bear to look at him. He reminded me of what my selfishness had caused. He told me that we had hurt Leila and that my babies were gone. I pulled my hand away and turned away from him. He tried to talk to me all day, but I blocked him out and pretended to sleep. Eventually, he left and I was able to cry while lying in bed alone with my regrets and emotions.

Each day Kieron came and each day I ignored him. After three days the doctor told me that I could go home. I hadn't seen Leila for days but I thought the experience had been quite traumatic for her and wasn't sure what I would have said to her, so I was grateful for the chance to avoid her. That afternoon Kieron came to take me home. When I walked in I was struck by the silence of the apartment. I looked around and noticed that Leila's bedroom door was open. Then it hit me. All her things were gone. I looked around in confusion then saw the shame etched upon Kieron's face. "Where is she?" I asked him, the first words I had spoken to him since he came back. He told me to sit down and explained what had happened on that fateful night when our babies died.

Kieron had come home and gone straight to the bookstore to meet me. After two hours of waiting, with no word from me, he had got worried and decided to turn up at my apartment under the pretext of visiting someone else in the building. When he got there, some of my friends were talking about me being taken out in an ambulance. He had rushed to the hospital. When he got to my room, he had seen me lying unconscious (still anaesthetised) and had rushed in frantically. He was so engrossed in checking me over that he hadn't noticed Leila's small frame curled up in the chair near the window watching over me like the loyal friend she was. It was only when he heard a sharp intake of breath behind him that he turned to see her face full of contempt and comprehension as all the pieces fell into place for her. He said that she didn't give him the chance to explain or say anything, she just stormed out. The next day she had left a note at the nurses' station explaining that she was changing school and moving and never wanted to hear from either of us again. I sat there listening in anguish and disbelief and felt numb. I couldn't muster up any more tears I just sat there motionless. After what seemed like hours, I noticed Kieron still sitting, watching me. I asked him to leave and give me some space. For the next month, I didn't leave the apartment except to take my exams. I locked myself away from the world creating a self-imposed exile. I didn't answer any calls and wouldn't allow any visits from anyone, including Kieron. I was punishing him and myself for what we had done to Leila and my inability to give life to my babies. On day 31 of my self-imposed exile, I heard a knock at my door. As usual, I ignored it and continued typing, determined to finish my diary entry for the day, but the person wouldn't go away. Finally, I shouted, "just go away, please!"

The response I got almost made me fall off my chair. "I'll leave when your funky ass opens the door!" There was no mistaking Lola's dulcet though abusive tones. I rushed to the door and wrenched it open, longing to let the smile I felt inside push to the surface but I still felt as if I didn't deserve to smile so I opened the door hugged her and sat back at the table in front of my laptop. Lola placed a box on the table next to me and said: "you know you never miss out on my birthday cake and it appeared that you didn't plan to pick up your share this year so here I am." "Your birthday?" I murmured. I had for the first time in my life forgotten her birthday and shame washed over me again.

I looked at her forlornly and said "that's just another thing I've screwed up! You have no idea what a mess I've made of things lately". In classic Lola style, her response was "Hold on while I grab a piece of this cake because this sounds like a long ass story". She then proceeded to cut my share of cake in two and sat in front of me munching away on it like it was the most natural thing in the world to eat the cake that's she had claimed was for me.

As I poured out my sorry tale, Lola sat there, not answering and not betraying any emotion. Once I was done, she said "I have three questions for you:

1. Is this why you haven't been speaking to the family?

2. Did you plan any of this?

3. Do you like feeling like this?"

I looked at her and said, "well yes, no and no". "Right then, next time you feel depressed and go through a life changing ordeal, please reach out to at least one of the family. There's no point in having eight siblings and still feeling alone in the world. Everyone has been worried about you but wanted to give you space to work things out by yourself. We each know how it can feel being part of such a big family so we figured that when you needed us, you would call but when you didn't, we knew something was seriously wrong. It was all I could do to stop Adam delivering the cake, ready to open up a can of whup-ass on the sap who had fucked his sister up – his words not mine! Because he seemed to know, it was something to do with a guy.

Also, I agree that you fucked up but it wasn't intentional and you can't continue living like this. The only saving grace is that your guilt made you an overachiever. I bet you don't even know that the results of your last two assignments were sent home because you didn't pick them up. You got distinctions in both and you're on track to gain a very decent Masters Degree. Pretty good for a little fuck up like you. I also have another letter which we didn't open I'll let you open that one later." As she finished her speech, she handed me a silver envelope from her bag with loping writing on the front that I recognised as Kieron's. I took it from her and tucked it into my dressing gown pocket to read later.

"You have approximately three weeks until graduation. What do you want to do with your life and where you intend to live? Lola asked, taking charge of my life as she always did. "Dad has an administrative posting in London so Mum, JoJo and Lucky are there. Tyrone and I have decided to make New York our permanent home so you're welcome to stay with us or you can join Adam. He's going back to Guyana to work with Ravin. Then again, another option is to go to the twins Jamaica or if you're totally feeling like an adventure, Vanessa and the kids are in Sri Lanka with Stephen. He's doing a special architecture project out there at the moment. The world was my oyster, but I didn't have the energy to make a decision. All I wanted to do was to take a quick nap.

Lola could read me like a book and said "You look exhausted" go and lie down while I cook us something. I'm going to be here for a few days to help you make a decision and make plans to move your stuff to wherever you decide to go." I smiled at her gratefully and folded her into a tight embrace, taking in her familiar smell and feeling so grateful to have her love and support.

In my room, I took the letter she had given me out of its silver envelope. It was indeed a letter from Kieron, explaining that he had been offered a job. It was everything he had ever wanted, but he would need to finish his degree through distance learning, he had intended to ask me to leave with him but after all, that had happened and me ignoring him he hadn't been able to tell me. He was gone. He had moved to Japan and abandoned me. Even though I knew that I had pushed him away, I still felt lost and abandoned. He had included a postal address where I could write to him and "begged" me to make contact when I was "recovered". He also told me how much he loved me and how special I was to him and ended the letter with a poem

"So fleeting were your little lives

No chance for me and mom

To meet you or to cherish you

So quickly you were gone

Cubs from a lioness I tried to tame

But after you, she's not the same

Time may heal but what's the deal

When all I want is gone."

As I wiped the tears from my face, I knew then, that I would never contact Kieron. We weren't meant to be together and we had paid the price for ignoring the rules of the universe.

MILES

After I had left University, I decided to go and party with the twins in Jamaica for a month before heading to London to start my real life. As a newly qualified HR professional, I struggled to find a job in my field so used the time to do some short courses in IT and re-establish links with Zee, who was studying alternative medicines in Edinburgh.

After two months of alternating between visiting Zee in Edinburgh and my parents' current home in London, I was offered a job as an HR manager with a venture capital consultancy firm. I was so happy to be getting a steady income because it meant that I could move out of my parents' home and rent a small place of my own in South London. I liked spending time with them but they were still tiptoeing around me after the miscarriage and I needed my own space.

I threw myself into my new job focusing on family and work. I had sworn off men after my experiences with Reece and Kieron and happily focused on building my reputation at the firm and spoiling Lucky and JoJo. One Monday morning I was handed a note as I walked into the office telling me that I needed to meet one of the acquisition partners at the coffee shop near our offices at 10am. I was intrigued. The infamous Miles Ellington didn't often mix with anyone outside the chosen few whizz kids that he picked every year to be part of his team and I was curious about what the meeting could be about. I slowly made my way to my desk to pick up my notebook, my mind racing with all the possible things that he could want to speak to me about.

At 9.55am, I walked into the bustling coffee shop and immediately saw Miles sitting in a booth at the rear of the shop, trying and failing, to look incognito in his expensive suit. I slid into the booth as he pushed a cup towards me; "It's caramel cappuccino" he said, "I took the liberty of ordering what I thought you would like". I accepted it gratefully. Any caffeine before 10am was a blessing and I wasn't going to tell him that he had guessed my mix correctly. I inhaled, took a long mouthful and set the cup down, to find Miles gazing at me in obvious amusement. "Right, I guess that you want to know why we are here? He said. "Well, I've been watching your progress in HR with some interest. You've developed quite a reputation as a maverick. Your unconventional yet thorough approach to people issues seems moderately effective and I would like to test whether your approach is down to luck or skill. I'm offering you a unique career opportunity; but before I set out that offer I need you to sign a confidentiality agreement". I took the document he had slid across the table, skimming its content while picking up the expensive pen he had also pushed across to me. It was a pretty basic agreement that stipulated that I didn't disclose any information about "Project Saturn" irrespective of whether I took up the job offer or not. I was extremely curious about the detail of "Project Saturn" so I readily signed the agreement, glad that the agonising wait for information was about to be over.

As I looked up from the document, I noticed Miles gazing at me intently again. As my eyes met his eyes, he averted them and began speaking. He explained that our company was soon to acquire a management consultancy firm and as a result of this acquisition, operations were being divided between two offices. One in New York and one in London. He had been offered and accepted the role of CEO of the London Office with carte blanche to create his own team from cleaner to board level through recruitment or retention of new and existing staff. He wanted a strong but innovative HR Lead for the London office and he wanted to offer me the job with immediate effect.

The acquisition wasn't finalised and would impact share prices hence the need for confidentiality. However, he intended to hit the ground running regarding negotiating new contracts and relocation deals with staff so wanted me to start reviewing staff profiles and developing a draft organisational structure to agree with him over the coming months. I would be reporting direct to him and due to the nature of the role, I would be working out of our new offices, overseeing their renovation as well as meeting him twice a week in the evenings to agree shortlists and contract terms. We would meet outside usual business hours to lessen any potential inquiry from other staff.

For five months I worked tirelessly, managing the office design and creating the new organisation. Miles and I met twice weekly in my new plush corner office, often ordering food while we thrashed out and debated job descriptions and shortlisted candidates. Often our sessions lasted into the wee hours of the morning and I sometimes teased him that his wife would wonder if he was having an affair, but he always shrugged off my comments saying that he was sure she wouldn't notice.

After working together for so long, we had developed an understanding of the other's style and ways of working. We knew what the other would want for dinner and I often pre-ordered his meal, so that it was waiting when he arrived or he would bring me snacks for late into the night. Finally, we were a couple of days from the announcement of the merger and we had everything ready. Miles suggested that we meet for a final debrief the night before the announcement as he wanted to finalise the bonus and performance framework. That day I was also called into a meeting at the Head Office to sign my official transfer papers so we agreed that we would meet back at my office a bit later than our usual 6pm.

At approximately 6.30 pm, I pulled up to our building in a taxi and got the lift up to my office. When I got there, I was astounded. My office had been redecorated. Rather than the standard furniture I had an oak desk with an antique globe on it and a beautiful mural was painted on my wall. I was astounded and I couldn't help but sink into my new work chair taking in the smell of new leather and enjoying how the London night lights sparkled through my window. As I took a minute to savour the newness and twirl in my chair, Miles walked in and said "I'm glad you like it. A little bird told me it was your birthday last week. I wanted to give you a reward for all your hard work and I thought that you would like the personal touches in your office as a birthday gift". I turned to him, my eyes glistening. I felt so choked up with emotion. For the past few months, I had put my heart and soul into this project and it felt so overwhelming to be recognised for those efforts. Without thinking, I bounced out of my chair and threw my arms around Miles murmuring "Thank you". In that split second I became acutely aware of his smell and just as I began to pull away, I felt his arms circle around me and squeeze me tightly before we both broke the embrace. For what seemed like an eternity we stared at each other awkwardly until I said "wow who'd have thought the great Miles Ellington was human" and we both laughed.

The next night was the launch. All the new directors were invited to a champagne reception in the lobby of our new building. I had a hectic day finalising details and ensuring that everything was ready for when the staff would arrive for their first day at work. At about 5pm I received a page from reception saying that my driver had arrived. I was thoroughly confused as I hadn't ordered a driver so I explained this to reception and continued going through my checklist. Within moments, my phone rang again. I grabbed it quickly and said "yes?" It was reception again, explaining that the driver was adamant that he was booked for me. "Fine, I'm coming down," I said. I secured my office and went down. When I got there, the driver introduced himself as Jim and handed me an envelope. In it was a note from Miles explaining that as part of my "bonus" he had arranged for me to go to the DKNY shop for a private viewing and to get an outfit for later. He also had an expert team to do my hair and makeup, who were waiting at the Hilton Hotel in the Executive Suite, which had been booked for me as part of the "bonus". Jim would then take me back to the office for the party and he would be available to return me to the suite to stay overnight after the party and then take me home the next morning.

I was awestruck. I quickly ran to my office, picked up my bag and jacket and flew out of the office. I sat back in the car feeling shocked and elated and vowed to take notice of every single detail so that I could share it with Zee the next time that I spoke to her. I pulled up to Donna Karan's flagship store and loved that the staff greeted me by name. I was led to a private dressing room, given some free champagne and told to pick out as many dresses as I liked. I chose ten dresses and tried them on, in turn, twisting and turning as I viewed myself in the multiple mirrors and wishing that I had someone I trusted to get advice from.

After dress number ten, I still felt like something wasn't

quite right so Tanya, my personal sales assistant, went away and spoke to some colleagues. When she came back, she was smiling like the cat that got the cream. She had a new dress for me to try that had just arrived and wasn't even on the shelves yet. As soon as she unsheathed it, I knew I had to have it. It was black satin with a detachable back zip clip which you could customise with your initial. I chose the letter zed and tried it on. It was fabulous and I was able to get matching alphabet shoes and earrings. I hurried back to the car making a quick stop at Starbucks to get some coffee for Jim before we made our way to the hotel. At the hotel, I told Jim I would be about an hour getting ready and suggested that he get some dinner and charge it to my room. He smiled and said "you really are a diva aren't you?" and I laughed as I skipped away to get the lift to my room.

When I got there, the stylist and a makeup artist were waiting for me as promised in Miles' note and I settled down for some pampering. I got prepared in the lap of luxury feeling incredibly special. By the time I glided into the reception, I felt like a million dollars and I apparently looked it, judging by the appreciative stares that some of the associates were throwing my way. I also bumped into some of my old colleagues who had been offered new jobs in the London office. It was a great evening, filled with networking and getting to know clients and the New York colleagues as well as the new recruits.

I spotted Miles a couple of times and tried to get to him to thank him for the gift experience but one or both of us kept getting caught in a conversation. It seemed impossible to find him so I gave up, planning to thank him the next day. With free champagne flowing all night and me drinking on an empty stomach it wasn't long before I felt a bit tipsy. I switched to water but somehow still kept getting glasses of champagne placed into my hands. At the end of the night, I swayed towards the front door to meet Jim, who would take me back o go back to the hotel. In the foyer of our building, I felt a hand on my arm guiding me towards the doors. I turned and saw it was Miles and smiled at him as I leant into him trying to manage my sway. "Hmm someone had fun tonight!" he said while smiling lazily at me. "Yes it was all like a dream, Thank you so much!" I replied. He guided me into the back of the car and closed the door behind me and then went around and slid in on the other side. I looked at him in vague surprise and he laughed saying that he was also booked into the hotel so thought he would grab a lift.

I sank into the seat, slipped my shoes off and said: "wow high heels really hurt, despite how good they look". As I slumped there, giggling, feeling tipsy and on top of the world, Miles said to me quietly "put your feet up and get comfy. We've hit some traffic". I complied, putting my feet up between us. I was extremely surprised when he moved my feet into his lap and started to massage them slowly but firmly, "Mmm that feels nice" I said as I drifted to sleep. The next thing I knew Miles was shaking me gently saying "we're at the hotel sleeping beauty". I jumped to attention and scrambled out of the car, forgetting that I was barefoot. Miles quickly came around to my side of the car and said "whoa there Cinderella, I think you forgot something" and dropped my shoes onto the kerb next to me. As I struggled back into the heels he waited patiently, then we walked into the hotel lobby where I promptly stumbled on the marble floor and twisted my ankle. I fell in a dishevelled heap on the floor feeling foolish and clumsy. I looked up at Miles forlornly and was slightly pissed off to see him trying not to laugh while failing miserably. As I watched him chuckle, I couldn't help but laugh too and soon we were both in an uncontrollable fit of giggles while other guests looked at us in confusion. After a few minutes, Miles composed himself enough to suggest that he help me up and to my room and I was grateful for his strength as I limped to the elevator.

Once we got to my room, I thanked him and assured him that I would be okay. He explained that he was in the room below mine 101 and that I could call him if I needed anything. I thanked him again and shut the door, ready to relax in the bath and watch TV. I ran a hot bath, put on a plush bathrobe and then found that the TV in the bathroom was unplugged and I couldn't reach the plug with a sprained ankle. I really wanted to watch TV so I bit the bullet and called Miles asking him to come and help me plug the TV in. He laughed and said "sure" and within moments, he was knocking at my door.

When I opened it I was blown away. There stood the great Miles Ellington in grey sweatpants and a t-shirt with his salt and pepper hair curling damply at the nape of his neck. I hadn't noticed how disarmingly attractive he was and despite the 20 year age difference I felt my heart skip a beat. *It must be the champagne* I thought and tried to ignore the butterflies in my stomach as I showed him into the bathroom acutely aware that I was only wearing a bathrobe. He quickly plugged in the TV and suddenly the room was filled with the mellow sounds of Babyface singing my favourite song "Anytime". Without thinking, I shut my eyes and started swaying and humming the song. Suddenly I felt strong arms around me and Miles whispered in my ear "I love this song too". His warm arms around me reminded me of how long it had been since I had been held by a man and I welcomed his embrace. As we swayed to the song, his hands started to roam my body and I felt like I was being transported to a utopia where every touch set my skin alight with fire and longing. He turned me around to face him and kissed me hungrily. I thought to protest but the thought left my mind as desire engulfed me. I was so caught up in the moment that all I could do was savour and enjoy every minute.

The intensity of the kissing increased and became more urgent. It was like I couldn't even remember my own name. He kissed the way he did business, forceful and confident and I felt his hands tugging at the string of the bathrobe, pulling it apart. In my mind, I knew I should say no. He was married and my boss but it felt too good. If I was completely honest, I had wanted Miles for a long time and it felt fitting that part of my reward for all my hard work should be this one indescribably pleasurable indiscretion.

Miles' mouth had left mine and he was now kissing my neck expertly while massaging the skin just below my breasts. I couldn't believe how aroused he was making me without even touching my breasts. Then his mouth travelled further down, pulling at my nipples one by one. Skimming them with his teeth and slightly nibbling them. I let out an involuntary moan because this was so damn hot. But Miles had more in store for me. He started kissing me again, assaulting my tongue with his, invading my mouth and taking control.

As he kissed me, he guided me across the room to the desk which stood near the window., I couldn't believe that this was happening. As I looked at the twinkling of the London skyline, I smiled wondering how many other trysts were happening in the sparkling buildings. As my legs bumped against the desk, Miles resumed kissing my neck, working his way down to my nipples, stopping briefly to nip at them before continuing his journey down my stomach. By now, his fingers were massaging my clitoris. Slowly and deliberately he moved his fingers in and out of me, while his thumb rubbed slowly on my clitoris, spreading the lips to allow him to follow it as it retreated.

I let out a cry. It was excruciatingly pleasurable but so intense at the same time, especially now that he was applying pressure to my g spot. When I felt the coolness of his tongue on my clitoris I thought I was going to faint, so much so, that my knees actually buckled. He laughed as he lifted his head and stood up. "Let's make this more comfortable," he said, and lifted me up, effortlessly placing me on the desk and telling me to lie back with my legs up. I looked at him confused and said: "what are you doing?". "Hmm," he said, "you know that I like late night snacks. Well, I'm just about to have a midnight feast!"

I was confused, wondering why I was lying here on the desk if he was about to go eat. Frankly I felt a bit stupid. He looked at my face and smiled. Then in a flash, he sat down on the chair next to the desk, wheeled it between my legs and gave my clitoris a long lick. "Hmmm," he said, "this is one of the sweetest snacks I've ever had". Despite the sexy atmosphere, I let out a giggle at my own confusion. "Did someone say something amusing?" he said from between my legs. "I think I need you to take me more seriously," he said while inserting his finger into me again and starting a relentless rhythm of pressure on my clitoris and g-spot while licking me. I could feel myself building to an orgasm, that familiar pressure cooker sensation was hard to deny. As it got more intense I started to mumble, Miles, Miles, Miles, I couldn't stop myself I started to cum all over his mouth and hand. "That's right baby," he said "let go for me. You're way too uptight sometimes". I couldn't even disagree with him or question what he meant because I was in the throes of the most intense orgasm I had ever experienced.

As the feeling subsided, Miles pulled me into a sitting position and kissed me, ensuring that I tasted the musky flavour of my own juices as they were smeared all over his mouth and tongue. Then he said to me "how long has it been for you?" "About a year" I stammered assuming he was asking about my last orgasm. He raised my face so he was looking me in the eye and said: "are you sure?" "Yes," I said earnestly. "It's complicated, but suffice to say I was off men for a while." "Hmm," he said, "good!" and he returned to kissing me intensely. As we kissed, he took my hand and placed it in the band of his sweatpants. I took the hint and started to play with his stomach right above the band, then I took both my hands and pushed them into his trousers.

I was surprised to feel his hard erection already right at the top of the waistband, he was rock hard, I clasped the shaft and slowly rubbed it up and down, "hmm that feels good Ms Fraser" he said, "I swear I want to be in you right now". He pulled me off the desk and swept me up in a kiss, which he quickly broke as he turned me around and planted kisses on the back of my neck and on my back. Nibbling and biting while snaking his hands around to cup my breasts and squeeze my nipples. With an air of authority, Miles pushed my body forward and his hands moved from my breasts. Before I could protest, I felt him thrusting into me with a ferocity that made me catch my breath. Even though I was wet from my recent orgasm and his attention, I still felt like he was ripping me open. A year without sex, as well as his girth, took some getting used to and there was nowhere to run as I was bent over the desk. He kept up a rhythm inside me, in and out, in and out with the occasional grind to get himself deeper embedded in me. For the second time, I felt the familiar sensation of pressure and I started to moan again urgently saying "Miles I think I want to cum". "Well, cum then baby. Nothing is stopping you. Cum right over my cock. Don't hold back. I want to feel your walls contract on me and all your juices spilling on me" he growled in my ear.

The sound of those words coming out of his mouth pushed me over the edge. I started to thrust my hips backwards to meet him. Harder and faster like I was riding the biggest wave. "Aaaah yes baby. That's it. Harder. That's it. Push it back" he said as he gripped my ass and squeezed. "Argh, I'm about to cum too baby. That's it. Don't stop." he said as he thrust himself deeper and deeper into me. I felt pleasure and pain all rolled up into one. As I started to cum, I let out a long wail. I felt him tense before he also let out a long sigh. "Simultaneous orgasm the first time. Wow" I said. He chuckled and started to withdraw from me while pulling me up. "Shower time I think," he said. I felt a little self-conscious, but I think I would have felt weirder bending down to pick up my robe, so I walked with him into the bathroom. As I walked behind him, I noticed that he had stepped out of his sweat pants and was pulling his t-shirt over his head. *Oh shit,* I thought *he is going to shower with me.* I walked over to the shower cubicle and turned on the water before stepping in trying to act nonchalant when Miles stepped in behind me.

Then I felt his mouth on my neck again. As he leant behind me, he took the shower head down, raining water all over himself and me while being careful not to wet my hair too much. "Open your legs" he whispered and I obliged unthinkingly. He fiddled with the shower head and then placed it between my legs, using a strong stream of water to massage my throbbing clit with cold water. I jumped and he laughed and said: "feels good?" "Uh-huh," I said "very good", He washed me off and then removed the head and adjusted it again so that warm water cascaded my body. Then he reached around replaced it on the wall and said "which shower gel?" holding up the two that I had left in the bathroom earlier. "Strawberries and cream please," I said. "Hmmm, good choice," he said, putting the other bottle down and squeezing some into his hand. As he lathered it up, I thought to myself that this felt almost too good to be true. He rubbed my shoulders with the shower gel. It was so sexy, the smell of strawberries and him rubbing my skin. When I was soaped all over, he said: "my turn now". He chose coconut and handed me the bottle. I had never showered with a man before so I was a little apprehensive but I tried to appear as if this was

116

completely normal. Squeezing gel into my hand and then rubbing his shoulders, "ooooh cold" Miles said. "It's customary to lather the gel in your hands first you know Zavia. Saves the other person having the shock of ice cold gel on their back!" "Oh sorry!" I said. He laughed and grumbled, "it's ok just don't do it next time".

Next time I thought and smiled. I would love to have a next time with this man. Once he was all soaped up, he turned me around and kissed me pressing our bodies together so the soap made us slide against each other. We stayed like that, kissing and sliding while the water from the shower slowly washed all the soap off us. Once all the soap was gone I decided to give him a treat of my own. Right there in the shower I bent down and kissed the head of his penis. He looked at me and smiled while I played with the head in my mouth. Slowly licking the tip and swirling it around with my tongue. "I think we should get out of here before you mess all your hair up" he said. I straightened up and smiled as he stepped out of the cubicle and then reached to help me out.

As we stood in the bathroom, I wasn't sure what to say or do. He handed me a towel and said: "dry your skin or else you will catch your death of cold". I complied, while he left the bathroom with a towel wrapped around his waist, I was still shocked about his physique. It was hot for a man of 45 and his sexual skills showed that he had spent much of those 45 years learning the art of pleasing a woman. "What are you doing in there?" he said. I'd apparently been wrapped up in my thoughts and drying myself for longer than I appreciated. I wrapped myself in a towel and stepped into the bedroom. he was laying on the bed without his towel. "Come over here," he said, "I think you started something that you need to finish". I smiled and blushed slightly when I noticed his erection. Then found my courage and boldly dropped my towel, walking over to the foot of the bed naked. His eyes glinted, a sign that he had something in mind. I had learnt that from watching him negotiate at work. I crawled onto the bed and started kissing his legs from his ankles upwards. Planting small kisses on his calves, doing them one side at a time and slowly working up. As I got to his inner thigh, I spent some time nibbling, making circles with light kisses. "Hurry up and get to the point Zavia!"

he said impatiently. "I'm dying with anticipation here".

A knock at the door interrupted me and he sighed, "bad fucking timing" he said as he got up off the bed. You're naked Miles" I said. "I know," he said "it's no big deal. Trust me". I shook my head and turned onto my stomach on the bed. I heard Miles open the door and say "thanks a lot, Jim. You're off duty now. Sorry, I had to disturb you. I'll text you to let you know when I'm ready". I wasn't sure what Jim said, but Miles chuckled and then shut the door.

A second later, Miles strode back into the room with a bottle of champagne and two glasses. "Did you seriously get Jim to bring you up champagne and then answered the door naked?" I asked incredulously. "Of course, I didn't answer the door naked. There's a robe in the other room remember!" "Oh yes," I said laughingly. He shook his head and said, "sometimes I wonder about you." I giggled and said, "I'm not sure I need more champagne." "Well I do", he said and "you only need to have one glass". "Why?" I said. "You'll see", he replied.

He opened the bottle and I covered my ears and closed my eyes, hating the sound of the pop. I only opened my eyes when he nudged me with a glass. I took a small sip while he gulped down a mouthful. He stood at the foot of the bed looking at me and told me to move so I was sitting at the edge of the bed. I shuffled into position, wondering what would happen next. "Take a mouthful of champagne" he commanded, "but don't swallow it". I complied and then he said, "now put me in your mouth". I opened my eyes in surprise, and he said "Yes Zavia. I want you to give me a Champagne Shower." I looked him dead in the eye and then guided the head of his penis into my mouth, bathing it in the cool champagne. "Aaah! Yea baby! I heard him say. "That feels good. Do your magic". I moved my head up and down on him, swirling the champagne around the head and slowly sucking on him. "That's it Zavia. Suck that dick baby." He moaned.

His dirty talk heightened my arousal and I started to suck with increasing intensity. "Yes! Yes!" he kept moaning, and then he put his hands in my hair and pulled my head away from him.   By now the champagne was finished and he ordered me to take another mouthful. I did as I was told and we kept up this routine until my glass was almost empty. With the last mouthful, he built the intensity by controlling my head movements, his fingers entangled in my hair. I could feel him getting even harder which I thought was almost impossible. Then he suddenly pulled out of my mouth and pushed me back onto the bed, positioning himself between my legs. He looked at me and then thrust deeply into me, holding my hands above my head so I was a virtual prisoner to his thrusts. He kept up a relentless pace of pushing into me, then pulling out and then back in, until I was on the brink of orgasm. Then he stopped and said, "I don't want you to cum just yet". "Are you kidding?" I said "please Miles. I need to release. Please!" I whimpered. "Beg me harder", he said. "Tell me how much you want it". "I want it a lot!" I replied. "Do you want anyone else?" he said. "No," I said. "No who" he demanded. "No Miles. I don't want anyone else. I want you to fuck me". I said pleadingly. "Good" he responded. "I'm the only man who gets to fuck you from now on. You know that right?" "Yes", I said, willing to say anything if it got me an orgasm. "Good," he said as he thrust into me even deeper. With that thrust, I was pushed over the edge and I started to babble incoherently and my body released the pent up orgasm. Just as mine subsided, I felt Miles' muscles tighten and as I held his ass I felt him release inside me with an anguished moan. A moment later he twisted our bodies so we were side by side and he snuggled up to me and said: "sleep time, I think, Zavia".

The next morning, I woke with a terrible headache but a clear recollection of the fantastic day and night before. I stretched lazily and felt a stirring next to me. Miles' face was just inches away from mine. He watched me as I watched him and then kissed me on the lips and said "good morning sugar". I was shocked, to say the least, and immediately pulled away. "Sugar? How can you call me that? I admit that last night was fantastic, but pet names and morning kisses are hardly appropriate for work colleagues or more to the point my boss!" I said with raised eyebrows.   "Especially not my MARRIED boss!" I said emphatically.   Miles smiled enigmatically and said "why not? You are the most attractive, smart, enchanting woman I've ever met and I enjoy being with you. I want us to explore this connection that we have. After all, we may never feel this way again and life is too short." "But what about your wife?" I said. Even the words made me flush with shame that I had allowed this to happen. "My wife is none of your concern Zavia. She and I lead separate lives but you can imagine that the financial implications of divorce make it an extremely unattractive proposition for me until I am sure that I want to commit fully to another relationship.

Honestly until you, I never met anyone that made me even think about. Can't we just see how it goes and then decide the next steps? Get to know each other and enjoy each other without the glare of our colleagues? He asked plaintively. I wanted to say no but after Kieron, I had struggled to make an emotional connection with anyone and Miles seemed to represent security and devotion. I loved the way he had made me feel the day before and I respected him professionally which was also important to me.

So despite my initial misgivings I nodded and leant in to kiss him. As we broke the kiss, he got up and said he had to attend some briefings and would check in with me during the day as I had a couple of days off. He left me a package and a note on the table before he left. As soon as I heard the door bang shut, I ran and grabbed the bag off the table. Inside were two boxes. I was horrified to see that the first box was the morning after pill. I quickly scanned the note which said *"Good morning Zavia,*

As a man who doesn't take risks lightly, I ask that you take the pill and then make an appointment to go on a more regular form of contraception. This is the number of a GP friend of mine 020 8654 4389 if you would prefer not to use your own doctor. He won't be surprised to get your call should you decide to use him.

Also, seeing as you are mine now, please see a gift of my appreciation in the second box.

ME

I frowned feeling somewhat out of my depth. I had never had someone else instruct me to take medicine of any sort. Much less such a personal type. I was curious about the other box and was stunned to find a charm anklet in it with Miles' initials mixed with my own and various other charms. It was truly beautiful. While I was admiring it in its box, I popped the pill into my mouth and went looking for some water to wash it down.

I also picked up the phone and dialled Miles' number. "Yes Zavia," he said smoothly. "How do you know I'm not on the pill already and when did you have time to get the morning after pill and why couldn't I just get it myself?" I blurted it out all in one go. "You haven't had sex for a year, so I assumed that you didn't need regular contraception and I didn't leave the room. Jim brought the pill for me and I just wanted to give you one less thing to think about" he said. "Hmm", I said. "On that note," he asked, "have you taken it yet?" "No, I've decided not to take it," I said playfully. "Zavia," he said coldly "that is not the answer I expected. I seriously suggest that you rethink your response and call me back when you've changed your mind" then he slammed the phone down on me. I was shocked. Miles had turned on me quickly and ferociously.

I panicked, scared that I had offended him and redialed his number and said "I was kidding. I took the pill". "Thank you Zavia. You have to understand that I require you to have a clear understanding of my position and to stay on the same page as me. Jokes like that won't be tolerated". "Ok, Miles", I said meekly. "Good girl" he replied soothingly. Obviously placated for the time being. "I'm just on my way to a meeting and then Jim will be back to collect you and take you home in the next hour." "Thank you", I said gratefully. "No problem" he replied and clicked off the phone. I wasn't sure where I stood with him, but I know I wanted to be more than just his colleague. To please him I decided to call his friend, the doctor, and set up an appointment for on my way home. Dr Kenny sounded very kind on the phone and after our discussion, we agreed that the "depo" injection would be the best form of contraceptive. He agreed to fit me in within the hour so I hurried to get ready so that Jim could take me there and then take me home.

Later as I left the doctor's office, I texted Miles to let him know and was pleased when my phone buzzed in response. I fished it out and found a message from Miles saying

"good choice on the injection! No pesky periods to interrupt us. ME x

I smiled, glad that he approved and pleased that he had confirmed that I wasn't just a one-night stand.

As soon as I got home, I logged onto MSN Messenger and told Zee about all of the developments. I conveniently left out the fact that Miles was married but explained everything that had happened the night before. She was excited and wanted to meet him the next time we were all in the same country. She also told me all about Reuben the new guy she had met while in Anguilla, her current location. She explained that he was deep, some kind of hippy type and they had spent a lot of time debating history, theology and spiritualism. From the sounds of it, she was smitten.

She explained that he was Guyanese and intended to relocate to Guyana within the year. It seemed like she was thinking of following him, if things worked out, which would mean that finally she would settle down in one place. We signed off after swapping respective boy stories. Then I started the long job of tidying up and catching up on personal filing and emails which had been neglected while I prepared for the acquisition.

I was engrossed in responding to a message from Lola when I heard my buzzer go. I looked outside and saw a delivery van. I buzzed him up and was surprised to be handed a box and asked to sign for it. The driver went away while I eagerly opened the pink package. Inside was a card from Miles with the words good luck on your new job and inside was a monogrammed pink leather case, which held a laptop, initialled notepaper and a matching pen. It was perfect. I smiled and sent him a message to say thanks.

And so it went on for the next six months. Miles and I would travel together for work. We would meet in secret locations always arriving and departing separately. He showered me with gifts. After a trip to New York where he had met Lola and the twins, he said that he had a surprise for me, which involved a diversion from the route back to my building. Suddenly we stopped in front of a gorgeous house nestled in a quiet cul-de-sac, which was like an oasis in the busy streets of North London. He opened the door and explained it was a property he had recently acquired. As we walked in, I was stunned by the bright and airy space being presented to me and when we got to the garden I had to confess that I wished the house was mine. As I said it, Miles chuckled and explained that he had bought it for us. Our names were on the deeds and I could move in once I had hired decorators to get it ready. I was ecstatic. I couldn't wait to start decorating. That afternoon I went online and ordered some paint swatches. I also contacted some decorators and arranged to interview them on the following Saturday to decide who I would hire.

That week, I floated around the office like I was on cloud nine. Lydia, one of the new HR business partners, even commented on how happy I looked, I explained that I was moving house and getting caught up in the decorating. She chuckled and said "It must be in the air. I hear that that Mr Ellington has just bought a new house for his family, to make space for the new additions". As she said it, my heart skipped a beat, "new additions?" I said hoping that my voice didn't betray the rising panic that I felt. "Yes," she said as she busied herself with her filing. "His wife just had twins and they need more room, so they've moved to a big house in Hertfordshire. It means he'll have to stay in town more when he is working but lucky thing. She's got a new house, a nanny and a housekeeper I hear!"

I was horrified, and as fast as I could, I wandered back into my office, concocted a story about a migraine and asked Jilly my PA to cancel all my meetings for the day. I made my way home in a daze and cracked open a bottle of wine. I sank onto the sofa and sent Miles a message asking him to call me. Two hours, six texts and five glasses of wine later Miles text me back to say he couldn't talk but would catch up with me in the office. I text back saying I was feeling ill so had come home sick. He responded to say he would be going home that night and would call me at home the next day.

I lay there feeling so isolated. I couldn't tell anyone about how I felt because no one knew he was married so I just had to lie there imagining him playing happy families with his wife and children. When the images got too much, I let the anger take over and got up and ripped up all the colour samples and ideas I had written for redecorating "our" house on my mood board. I felt angry and betrayed. That night, I slept fitfully. I tried to change the subject in my mind but it proved difficult and at 4am I decided to just stare at the ceiling until I drifted off to sleep.

At 10am, I was still in bed when my phone rang. I noticed it was Miles' private number that he only used to call me. I answered hurriedly and blurted out "Why did you lie? You and Justine have just had twins but you said you aren't together. That it is just a sham marriage, but you bought her a house. She has a nanny and a housekeeper. I hate you why did you do this to me, make me a fool?" All my emotions came tumbling out and as I finished my tirade I heard him take a deep breath and sigh. "Are you done?" He asked. "I am not going to be spoken to like that. When you calm down, I will explain the situation. Don't call me unless you're calm" and then the phone went dead. I sat there in shock and disbelief and then dissolved into tears. What could I have done to deserve such bad luck? I got out of bed, wandered down to the kitchen and opened the fridge. I looked inside and pulled out a bottle of champagne that Miles had left there, picked up a coffee mug and curled up on the sofa drinking champagne and crying. The combination of the champagne, my emotions and my sleepless night must have sent me to sleep because the next thing I knew I heard the front door slamming shut and saw Miles striding into the room.

I stared at him wearily, not knowing whether I was in for another tongue lashing or not. He came in, sat down on the sofa next to me, put his arms around me and said "Zavia, why can't you trust me? I bought us a house because I knew I would be staying in town more and wanted us to have our own space. The twins were conceived nine months ago which means that you and I hadn't even started. Do you remember that I was out of the office for two weeks last year? Well, Justine and I went on a trip to try to make a last ditch attempt to fix our relationship. It didn't fix us but she fell pregnant on the journey. I've got her a housekeeper and nanny because when I leave her, she will need help with the four kids. I promise it's over between her and me" he said earnestly.

As I looked into his slate coloured eyes, my shoulders sagged in relief and I let out a breath I didn't even know I was holding. "Oh Miles," I said, "I'm sorry I doubted you." "It's ok baby," he said. "I know that you have trust issues and I forgive you". That night he stayed with me and we started a new mood board for the house. I also managed to catch up on work so my emails were up to date and I rearranged some meetings that I had missed. The next morning he was gone before I woke up and had left a note to say that he had to take his eldest daughter to a riding lesson and would speak to me later. He also said he trusted me to choose the right decorator and décor for the house as he wouldn't make the meetings with potential decorators that afternoon. I smiled at the kisses on the note sniffed it to catch a whiff of his scent and grabbed a cup of coffee from the pot he had left on for me.

On Monday when I got to the office I was surprised to see Paula settled in Jilly's chair, I looked at her quizzically and she laughed explaining that there was a new approach to ensuring information management and corporate memory which involved rotating PA's across the senior leaders to make sure that everyone was interchangeable. I smiled and said "Ok" and was happy when she assured me that she had had a seamless handover with Jilly. As I settled behind my desk, I noticed a message from Miles pop up on my phone. It said

"now that you are going to be overseeing the decorating at the house I have taken the liberty of completing a remote working request for you so that you can work from home most of the time with just occasional visits to the office, it's all been approved so you can start effective next week."

I was thrilled. I couldn't believe he had been so thoughtful and looked forward to more flexible days and less travel while having the opportunity to plough my energy into the decorating.

Three months later, the house was ready for us to move in. Miles said that as the twins were so young, we couldn't yet go public with our relationship but to celebrate our fresh start he wanted us to buy lots of new things. We went away for a shopping weekend where he bought lots of suits and clothes saying he wanted to look good for me and I happily arranged all our purchases into his wardrobe and the relevant parts of the house. I arranged to take a week off work and got the movers in so I was able to move all my stuff into the house at my own leisure. I arranged a grand housewarming for my friends and family and Miles, as usual, was a charming host. We even got my mum and dad to come over for a break and I was in my element. If anyone found it strange that Miles often rushed off at short notice or didn't sleep at the house some nights, then they were too polite to ask and I had already explained to my mother that his job was very hectic.

When I questioned his frequent absences, he told me that the twins were very demanding and it was his responsibility to keep his other two daughters amused and feeling valued. SO that Justine could focus on the twins. Although I wasn't happy about it, he pointed out that when we had a baby, I would want the same support. To hear him talk about our baby made me so happy that my heart swelled.

My days were filled with working at home, cooking and taking care of our home. Miles would come "home" from Tuesday to Thursday and would try to visit on a Saturday or arrange outings for us some weekends.

As my 25th birthday approached, I started to feel like I wanted to have a child. Zee had visited with her new husband Reuben and my gorgeous godson Jacob and I yearned for the unconditional love that I witnessed between the three of them. After they had left, I broached the topic with Miles. He explained that we would need to wait until the twins were at least three so that he could focus on our little person.

About three weeks before my birthday an old friend from, Lisette, came to London and sent me a quick message suggesting that we meet up. She was on a tight schedule so could only meet that day. I quickly jumped out of bed where I had been enjoying a lazy Tuesday morning of working and reading in bed. I grabbed a shower, got dressed and ran out. I had forgotten how impulsive Lisette could be and we were soon sitting on a train bound for Manchester so that I could see her modelling in fashion week. I didn't remember that Tuesday would mean Miles was home and I didn't think it mattered anyway. I watched Lisette in her show and then we went out clubbing. It was so nice letting my hair down. I couldn't remember the last time that I had danced the night away. Before I knew it, the club was closing and it was 3am. Lisette had a driver so we decided to drive back to London straight away so we could sleep in the car and take advantage of the clear roads. It was 5am when we pulled up in front of my house.

When we pulled into the driveway, I noticed that the curtains were moving in the front room so I hurriedly kissed Lisette goodbye making her promise to keep in touch and rushed into the house looking forward to seeing Miles. As I rushed towards swaying slightly due to tiredness and alcohol he turned and I saw that he was stony-faced. "Where have you been all night?" he said coldly. "I went to Manchester with my friend Lisette and then we went out to celebrate and my battery died". "Who the fuck is Lisette?" He roared, making me jump. "Are you sure that it was Lisette and not some guy that you've picked up with?" I looked at him shocked, "No, it really was Lisette", I said. "You can call her to see if she is real if you want". "No, it's fine," he said. "I just wondered who gave you permission to gallivant all night. You're my woman" he said. "Not some street walker. I expect better from you. Also, I don't even have a shirt ironed for my meeting this morning. If you weren't ready for this type of life, you should have said. I wouldn't have bothered to buy this house. Oh and what exactly do you think I ate yesterday while you were out? I don't spend good money on this house and waste my time rearranging your working pattern just so I have to do this shit for myself! You're incredibly selfish and ungrateful". As he finished his tirade, my temper flared but was dampened by the niggling thought in the back of my mind that maybe some of what he had said was true. I was incredibly blessed to have the life that I had and I always needed to remember that I told myself. It was this thought that prompted me to apologise to him and offer to whip him up an omelette for his breakfast and to make an extra special dinner for him that evening. He didn't acknowledge my apology but instead said "I'm not sure if I will stay here tonight, we will see" and turned and walked upstairs.

While he was upstairs, presumably getting ready for work, I mixed the eggs for the omelette and decided to make him some pancakes as well. I was tired from the night before, but I figured I could sleep when he left for work and I would call in sick once he had left. "Zavia", I heard him shouting "come upstairs". I turned off the heat on the cooker and ran up the stairs. As I turned into the bedroom, I heard that the shower was still running "Yes Miles" I called out. "I need the purple shirt ironed and put the striped tie to match it on the chair". "Ok", I said meekly and went into the dressing room to iron his shirt and pull the tie out. Luckily it didn't take me long to iron so within a couple of minutes I was done. I laid the shirt and tie out on the chair in the dressing room and went back into the bedroom to tell him that they were ready.

When I walked into the bedroom, he was standing next to the bed naked and said: "Can you help me dry my back?" His tone had softened and I noticed that he was asking not demanding. "Sure," I said amiably and went to wipe his back. As I approached him, I saw that he had an erection. I looked down at it wordlessly and he smiled, "I think you have some making up to do" he said and placed my hand on his hardness. I smiled back at him, glad that he appeared to have forgiven me. "You know what I like Zavia". "Yes I do," I said, as I knelt on the carpet taking him in my mouth. He moaned as my warm mouth engulfed him. "You know you belong to me," he said as he thrust his hips against my face. I tried to pull away but he held me in a vice-like grip, pleasuring himself as If I wasn't even there. As I struggled to breathe, I pushed at him and accidentally scratched him on the thigh. He pulled out of my mouth with a howl and said: "What the fuck Zavia?" "You were going too hard," I said "and you didn't seem to want to stop". "Surprisingly, I was enjoying it," he said derisively "but you messed it up. I'm not in the mood anymore". "Don't be like that?" I said touching his thigh. "No, it's cool. I have to go to my meeting now anyway" he said, pulling me to my feet. "You shouldn't turn me on so much," he said, "You make a man lose control". He kissed me on the cheek and said: "go make my breakfast or else I'll be late". I turned to leave the room and he playfully swatted me on my ass. I squealed and laughed as I left the room making my way to the kitchen humming.

That was the pattern between Miles and I. Flare-ups and then make ups. I was getting accustomed to it and attributed it to the fact that we were two very passionate people in love. I quickly finished the omelette and pancakes ready for when came downstairs. As he walked into the kitchen, my heart skipped a beat. He looked so attractive in his suit, already barking orders into his telephone about a new acquisition. He sat down and I placed a plate of pancakes in front of him with his omelettes, he grimaced at the pancakes and pushed them aside as he slammed his phone shut. "I can't eat all of this", he said bluntly and hurriedly stabbed his fork into his omelette. I poured him some orange juice and asked about the new acquisition. "It's a great opportunity. We are in negotiation stage but it looks very likely that we will get it. The new joined up organisation will be one of the biggest globally. I've been offered the role of CEO for the new group and now I have to review the resources. "Wow", I said. "I'll need to start coming into the office. That's a lot of staff". "Why would you need to get back into the office?" He asked. "I thought I was your HR lead?" I said quizzically. "Not for this," he said. I've been looking for an HR Director. I need someone more experienced. I am down to my final three choices and I will be interviewing them later this week.

"Oh", I said, feeling deflated. "Don't be disappointed" he said "You have a great job in one of the most successful global consultancy firms and you get to be a homemaker too. I've given you the perfect setup". "*Hmmm*", I thought starting to feel rebellious, but I quickly quelled the feeling reminding myself that lots of women would kill to be in my position.

Once he left I called Paula, explaining that I would be off that day as I was feeling under the weather. She said she hoped I felt better soon and I thanked her before clicking off. Then I jumped into the shower, setting the water on hot feeling the need to clear my head of all the conflicting thoughts and emotions.

Just as I climbed out of the shower, my phone rang. I ran into the bedroom and sat on the bed as I answered it. It was Lisette, "Wake up sleepy head," she said. "I'm not sleeping," I said. "The chance would be a fine thing". "What do you mean?" she asked "Come on, spill. What happened? I noticed the curtains twitching this morning when I dropped you off?" I started to tell her about my morning and then I found that the whole situation with Miles poured out, including the fact that Miles was married. It felt great unburdening myself about it. Lisette was a great friend and someone who never judged. She listened with the occasional exclamation or question until I fell silent. "Well Ok!" she said. "Do you want my honest opinion or the make Zavia feel better edition?" "The truth" I whispered knowing that Lisette's truth could often be extremely scathing. "I think you are fucking stupid for putting up with his bullying. If you paid as much attention to your career, you wouldn't need a man like him to give you money or a fancy house. That being he sounds sexy as hell so can I see why you fell into this trap, but if you intend to stay with him, you need to demand more. You say that you want a baby. Well, make that your bargaining chip. This set up seems to work for him, so it's time to make it work for you and if you aren't going to be having a baby get back in the career saddle! Because you being passed up for this new project means that you aren't a major player at work anymore either. You are at risk of losing everything my girl and it's time you balanced this shit out!" I smiled wistfully glad that she couldn't see my face. I could see where she was coming from, but I didn't know how to stand up to Miles. "Think about it, Zavia. You're going to be 25 in a few weeks and it's time to start thinking of yourself" she said. "Anyhow, that was my good deed for the day. I have a lunch date with one of the guys from last night. Poor fool is on the train coming to meet me, so gotta go and get myself ready. I leave tonight so see you the next time I fly in. Kisses and stuff" she said and put the phone down before I could respond.

Lisette was like a whirlwind, the complete antitheses to Zee. Where Zee was laidback and relaxed, Lisette was always doing something, always moving. I had met her just after college. After the incident with Kieron when I was partying in Jamaica and her energy had been a welcome distraction from my own thoughts. I loved getting caught up in her life so I could avoid my own and somehow we had developed a strong though intermittent bond.

That evening when Miles came home I had prepared all his favourite dishes and had a glass of cognac waiting for him as he walked through the door. I was dressed in one of his favourite colours and had decided to take Lisette's advice and work on the baby talk. I wanted a baby and now seemed to be the time to raise it, while things were looking positive for him. I know we had discussed the twins but I knew I was willing to do much of the parenting alone until he moved in with us and I would tell him so.

As he walked in, he smiled in appreciation and said "You look beautiful. You know I love that colour on you". He took a sip of cognac and said "Boy I needed that" as he loosened his tie. I had left some olives on the table for him as I knew that he liked to nibble on them as he drank and I busied myself in the kitchen adding the finishing touches to the dinner. "Go to the table" I called out to him, "I'm bringing dinner in". "Mmmm smells good," he said. "Yep! It's your favourite" I replied bringing in the lamb shank and laying it next to the shallot mash and roasted vegetables that were already on the table. "This looks fantastic Zavia," he said. "Thank you," I said beaming, glad that my plan seemed to be working. As we ate in companionable silence, I asked about his day and he said it had been good. He had brought home the final three CVs to prepare for the HR Director interviews the next day so he would be locked in the study for a couple of hours after dinner. "That's ok," I said, taking a deep breath. "So, erm, I've been thinking. I, erm, really want to have a baby and it seems like now would be a good time for us to start trying. He looked at me and said, "Why would now be a good time Zavia?" His calmness was slightly disarming so I continued. "Well I'm at a calm period in my career and you're about to get another high profile project. So if we planned it right, you would have

131

finished phase one, when the baby was born". He looked at me, narrowing his eyes as if thinking. "Ok then," he said. "We can start trying after your birthday because I have a surprise planned for you". I was elated and jumped up to hug and kiss him, looking forward to my surprise and the next phase of our relationship. After dinner, he went to the study and I cleaned the kitchen humming and feeling like I was on cloud nine.

A few weeks later it was my birthday. Miles had arranged for a private screening of a new movie about an unfaithful husband and a vengeful wife. The irony was not lost on me. As he watched the movie with me, I saw him smiling when the woman threw tantrums and I wondered if Justine was anything like that. Lisette was at the screening too having rearranged her schedule to surprise me and she cast me a few meaningful glances through the film which I studiously ignored. The evening included a champagne reception followed by dinner, As usual, Miles charmed everyone and paid particular attention to me, making me feel like a queen. I mingled with our friends after the film and swapped critiques with them about our favourite parts. Suddenly I felt my purse vibrating. It was Zee and her family calling to wish me a happy birthday. I left the main room and found a quiet spot between two giant statues near the toilets. I crouched down to get comfortable so that I could coo at my Godson over the telephone without anyone seeing or hearing me. As I finished the call, feeling happy and loved as well as a bit broody, I heard Miles and his friend Will laughing raucously. I was about to stand up until I heard Will say "I can't believe that Justine still doesn't know about this one. Usually, they don't last so long and you've even set up home with this one. You had better be careful or she will turn into the wife from the movie". Miles laughed and said "No way man. Justine is way too cool for that even if she did find out. She knows I am never going to leave her and the girls. Zavia is different I admit that. She's a good little homemaker and it beats staying in a hotel. Only thing is that she is talking about wanting a baby. I may have to promote her at work to get her mind off it. I'm not stupid, I think even Justine would probably freak out if I had a child with someone else. Can you imagine trying to juggle activities and parents' evenings? I have the perfect set up. I never miss important dates and I still spoil her and satisfy her. She has no reason to suspect that I have a bit on the side". Will laughed again and clapped Miles on his back and said: "I don't know where you get the energy, but anyway, let's go back in before Zavia notices we are gone".

Each word felt like a blow to my stomach. Somehow I stayed crouching until they had left. I had to get out of there. The walls were closing in and I felt like I was suffocating. I ran out into the foyer and ordered a taxi, looking around furtively hoping that no one saw me and asked where I was going. I couldn't face anyone at this moment. I had left a message at the reception for Miles explaining that I had an emergency call from my brother Adam which I had to go home to deal with. As I sat in the taxi crying uncontrollably, I dialled Adam's number, not caring that he was five hours behind me in Guyana. Once he answered, my sobs became uncontrollable and I was incomprehensible which forced him to start guessing what I was crying about. He asked if it was our parents or one of the others. Hearing how frantic he was becoming, I composed myself a little bit and reassured him that no one was hurt. My emotional state apparently conveyed to him that I needed him. He immediately said he would be on the next flight to London, but I needed some space to think so I suggested we meet in Amsterdam instead. I knew I couldn't face Miles in this state of mind. Once I had agreed on the plan with Adam, I sent Miles a text message explaining that Adam was in trouble and I needed to fly to Amsterdam to help him out so would need a couple of days off work. He immediately answered that it was all right and said he would get a lift with Will to his home in Hertfordshire as they were neighbours and he had a parent meeting the next morning that Justine couldn't attend. I texted *"cool"* and once I was home booked my ticket to Amsterdam.

I cried on and off all night, throughout the day and during the drive to the airport the next afternoon. By the time I got on the flight, I was all cried out and couldn't muster the strength to do anything except stare out of the window. As I disembarked, I got a message from Adam to say that he had just landed and would wait for me at the airport. I text back "Ok, I'm here now too" then went to find him in the arrival lounge.

When I saw him, I ran straight into his arms and started crying again. "Whoa, whoa. Sis you need to stop that girly nonsense and man up" he said. "You know that we don't act like sissies over anyone or anything in this family." Despite my distress, I laughed and punched him and we set off to find a taxi. As we pulled up to the hotel, Adam told me that I looked like a mess and he had no intention of being seen with me at the bar unless I fixed up. After we had checked in, I went to my room, had a quick shower, changed and put on some makeup. Finally, I felt a bit more human and ventured down to the bar where Adam was waiting for me. I smiled when I saw that he was sitting at the bar flirting with the manager and winked at me as she slipped him her number and I rolled my eyes. I sat at a table on the far side of the room and waited for him to come and join me. He brought over a bottle of Bacardi and a mug of juice and poured us both a drink. "So sis, tell me why we are taking this unscheduled trip? And why Miles left me a message saying that he hoped I was able to resolve my issue and reminding me to look after you?" he said with a raised eyebrow. "Did you tell him that I was the one who called you? I asked wearily. "No, of course not. I know the drill. Keep my mouth shut until I've spoken to you. How many times did that work for us when we were at school?" He said while chuckling. I gratefully accepted the drink that Adam had poured for me and let the whole story about Miles come tumbling out. I held nothing back from Adam, letting him into the minute details of my life with Miles. The more I told Adam the sterner his face became and the more it dawned on me that my relationship with Miles was controlling and unhealthy.

As I came to the end of my sorry tale Adam pulled out his phone and punched in a number "Charlie" he said "I have a little problem. I need your help with. How soon can you get to Amsterdam? I'll pay for flights and a room of course. He listened for a few moments, chuckled and ended the call. He then told me to contact the Executive HR Director and ask about what the transfer procedure would be if a member of staff wanted to change location. I quickly drafted an email and sent it off while asking him curiously who Charlie was. "Ha,

Charlie is my friend, Charles Ellis, a hot shot lawyer who specialises in messy divorce cases." "Divorce?" I queried, "why would I need a divorce lawyer? I'm not married" "No, you're not. But you live in a house purchased by your partner, in joint names so we need to understand what your legal standing is. I know that you love your house and presumably you don't want to pay Miles for his share?" I shook my head and said "No, I don't, so let's do things your way. I knew you were the best person to call".

Just then Adam got a message to say that Charles would be arriving in a few hours. When he arrived, we would convene a strategy meeting on how to extricate me from the hands of the bastard Miles but in the meantime, we had some time to kill. Adam suggested that we go and find some weed to smoke and I went along with him deciding that I probably needed to relax and forget about my problems for a while. A few hours later I was feeling pretty mellow as Adam and I went to meet Charles at the airport. I was pleasantly surprised to see a hot looking young guy step off the plane and stride towards us with a confident yet laid back smile. As he reached us, I was glad I had on sunglasses that hid my puffy eyes and allowed me to survey his body from head to toe which was a real treat.

We decided to go and get something to eat before talking to Charlie about things. Thankfully the food helped my weed-filled brain to clear and begin to focus so I was able to speak to Charlie without giggling and blurting out how cute he was.

Once dinner was over, we made some space on the table and decided on a plan of attack. I quickly outlined my perspective on things to him. "The papers for the house are in both Miles and my names but he pays the mortgage. I don't want his money, but I can't afford the mortgage alone and I don't want to lose the house. I also don't want to deal with Miles at work. I've sent a message to the Executive HR Director for some information about a potential transfer."

All the time that I was speaking, Charles was taking notes and intermittently chewing his pen while appearing deep in thought. Then he said, "Do you still love him?" "NO!" I shrieked. "No way!" I added emphatically. "So," he said, "you don't care how dirty this fight gets. You won't back down and take him back?" Before I could answer, Adam cut in and said "If she takes him back, the next case you're gonna need to deal with is my criminal defence. Because I'll kill her before, she lets herself be treated like that again!" I looked at Adam who was staring at me without even the glimmer of a smile and I gulped. "No I won't take him back," I said. "Good! Well, the next step is me calling Mr Hot Shot and outlining to him what I think will be a good settlement for you considering you are in most respects his common law wife. It isn't a legal term, but I'm betting that he won't want a protracted argument about things. He strikes me as someone who likes to get things done fast. I also want to convince him to support your request for an alternative work location and reporting line.

Unsurprisingly the call between Miles and Charles did not go well. The call was on speakerphone so I heard Miles roaring that no one fucked with him. He also told Charles that my work record was appalling and that I would be lucky to get a good performance review from him so I could kiss my career goodbye as well if I thought about telling anyone about our relationship. He also said he wouldn't be giving me the house unless I intended to buy him out. I couldn't believe that Miles was acting like this. I had done nothing but support him and believe his lies and now that he was caught he was turning on me. Finally, I saw him for the selfish man that he was.

The more I listened to the call the angrier I got. Finally, I interrupted the call and said "Miles, I just want this done. You hurt me so much and now I just want it to be over!" "Over?" he said "that's fine. You're flaky and I can't handle a flaky woman. We are done. I'll be putting all your shit in storage and you need to find somewhere else to play house from now on. Why don't you get your new man to finance you? You're obviously in Amsterdam fucking that lawyer guy". I laughed at the absurdity of the situation. "I am not fucking Charles," I said. I asked him to help me because I overheard you and Will talking the other night. On my birthday. You have no intention of leaving Justine. You lied to me". You lied to yourself Zavia. Haven't you heard the phrase actions speak louder than words? You knew I wasn't going to leave her and it suited you. You're just pissed off because I won't give you a baby."

I started to cry and left the room while Charles said "look, Mr Ellington, our terms are clear. Zavia wants a new job outside of your chain of command and she wants the house. It really is a small price to pay." "Fuck you" Miles screamed then the phone went silent before I heard the dial tone.

Charles knocked and came into my room and said "Ok Zavia. This isn't going to be easy. I suggest that you start looking for a new project citing a disagreement over your performance appraisal as the reason why you want to change jobs". "Ok", I said and opened my laptop to draft the email with Charles there. I hit send and was shocked when Verity, the group HR director emailed me back almost instantly. She said that she had received a similar email from Miles stating that we had failed to reach agreement on my performance review. As it happened, she had a short term project that required 6 months' maternity cover until the end of the year in a different office if I was willing to take it. I called her and accepted the assignment immediately and she asked when I could start. I told her whenever she needed me.

We agreed I would start on Monday as it was already Thursday and she would email me all the details. "There's just one more thing though", she said hesitantly. "Yes", I replied equally hesitantly. "This role will require you to be based n the office most days." "That's fine" I replied, relieved that it was something so minor. "Oh," she said, sounding surprised. "Why do you sound so surprised?" I asked. "Well, Mr Ellington has cited your refusal to come into the office as one of the reasons why he has given you an adverse performance rating" she replied candidly. "Oh ok": I said. "That's strange, he never mentioned that my working pattern was an issue for him before. But I can assure you I have no problem being office-based for this role. I'll be there bright and early on Monday morning". "Great," she said. "I'll let them know."

When I was sure that she was no longer on the telephone I turned to Charles and said: "The bastard is already on the offensive". "Sounds like it," he replied. "You know this won't be easy right Zavia?" He reiterated. "Yes I know," I said, "But it's the principle. I'm not giving up. He fucked with my heart and now he is fucking with my career he needs to pay". "Ok," Charles said. "Honestly, I never understood the attraction when Adam described you and Miles. You seemed way too beautiful and vibrant to be with an old fart". I laughed and said "Thanks, Charlie".

Adam and Charles decided to spend the weekend in Amsterdam as I had forced them to come, but I went back to London so that I could sort out where I would be staying while the battle with Miles was underway. I had asked Shawna, one of my cousins to pick me up some clothes from the house. She had spare keys in case of an emergency and I was glad that I had asked her before I spoke to Miles because who knew what he would do with my belongings.

Luckily for me, Shawna had a spare room and didn't mind me staying with her while I arranged to rent somewhere closer to my new office. I didn't want to spend too much on rent so was looking for a studio apartment. I couldn't believe my luck when Shawna told me that a studio would be available in her building within two weeks. Because Shawna recommended me to the letting agency, I was able to circumvent the long waiting times. When I arrived, Shawna tried to ask me about what had happened with Miles and the house, but I shrugged her off saying I would explain when I was ready.

On Monday morning, I reported to my new office. It was in London Bridge, so it was an easy commute from Norbury where Shawna lived. I had never worked in this part of the business before so there were lots of new people although there were some familiar faces including Jilly, my former assistant who had asked to be moved when I left. I was glad to see a familiar face and as she handed me a stack of papers, I needed to read, she squeezed my hand and said: "Never let a man define you". I looked at her in surprise and she said "I've been here for over 20 years. I've seen a lot of the goings on" and she winked. "I also have an envelope from Paula for you", she said. I took it from her but waited until she had left to read it. When I opened it, I found a typed note that said

"All your belongings are in a storage locker in Canary Wharf. Enclosed is the key. I have paid for storage for two months, then you're on your own".

Mr Miles Ellington III

I shrugged off the tears that pricked the back of my eyes at such an impersonal message from Miles and wondered what Paula had thought as he dictated it to her. But although I was upset I was also pissed off. I would make sure he paid for SCREWING me UP!

Here's a Sneak Peak of Screwed Up Sister – Part 2

How Does Zavia make him pay?..........

All will be revealed!

SCREWED UP SISTER – PART II (A PREVIEW)

After Miles, I was very wary of men. I spent my secondment to the London Bridge office focusing on rebuilding my career and reputation, which Miles had jeopardised with rumour and innuendo about my performance and professionalism. I also partied hard with Shawna, who was wild. I loved spending time with her. Life was always one big party for her and at 25, I was ready to rekindle my youth, which had been interrupted by playing house with Miles. To coincide with the end of my secondment, I would be going home to Guyana for Christmas. I need to relax, Miles was still dragging out the battle for the house and I wanted to unplug from everything for a while.

When I told Zee that I would be coming home for a month in December, she squealed in delight. It had been a long time since we were in one place for so long and most of my family would be home too, so I was really excited.

As I touched down in Guyana, I looked forward to the moment when I would step off the plane and experience the familiar feeling of humidity hitting my body. The moment the plane door opened I was rewarded with the wave of heat and I inhaled the smell that I can only describe as home. It was so good to be home and as the heat permeated my bones I could almost feel the stress start to dissipate from my body.

Two days later I was lounging by the pool at the Pegasus, one of Guyana's most prestigious hotels, where my family had a lifetime club membership. I was trying to nap in the warm rays of the sun when I felt a shadow being cast over my body. I assumed that it was someone walking through the loungers so expected it to move but after a few minutes it hadn't. I opened my eyes and pulled off my sunglasses to find an impossibly tall man standing over me. I was more than annoyed at this intrusion into my space. "Something I can help you with?" I said snootily. "No," he said "I'm just intrigued about why someone as beautiful as you are is lying here alone. Wondered if you wanted company?" I snorted impatiently and said "No it's fine. I like my own company". "Ok," he said and moved away. His lack of insistence surprised me, men were normally pushier. I was pleasantly surprised.

For the next week, I saw him almost every day in and around the hotel. I had no idea what he did there, but he always nodded at me without attempting to speak to me again. In a way, I was disappointed, but I was enjoying my own company so I didn't fixate on it. For once my family seemed to understand that I needed some "me" time. So although I saw them at home, they didn't press me to participate in the usual family stuff which really pleased me.

The weekend after Christmas, a few of us decided to go to the annual December Gala Dinner and Ball at the Pegasus. I booked a hotel room for the night so that I wouldn't have to worry about driving home. Adam had invited Charles over for Christmas so he would be there too and he had emailed me to say that he would update me on the latest position. Miles was still resisting every offer that Charles had made to resolve our situation. The longer he played hardball, the more I wanted to dig my heels in. *Fucking bastard* I thought. *How dare he fuck with me?*

This year's gala was a masquerade party. I was looking forward to seeing Charles again. I felt like maybe it was time to break my self-imposed vow of celibacy and Charles seemed like he would be a safe and grateful bet. I dressed in an impossibly short Greek style dress with a beautiful white mask. I made sure that the bed was turned down and that I had lingerie available just in case I was able to find a playmate for, later on, either Charles or someone else and then I went downstairs to make my grand entrance.

As I walked into the ballroom, I was amused to see that people had made a concerted effort to disguise themselves with masks of all different colours and hues. I looked around the room and quickly recognised Adam's frame alongside another guy who I assumed was Charles. I was jostling my way through the crowd to get to them when I was accosted by two tall masked men who each took one of my arms and twirled me along to the music. I jigged with them playfully and then excused myself to continue my journey to the bar. I was grateful for the anonymity that my mask afforded me and I was looking forward to letting my hair down in relative privacy.

When I finally got to the bar, I found that Zee and Daniel were there as well as the twins and my cousins Shawna and Rocco, who had flown in from London a couple of days after me. We bought a few bottles of champagne and then moved to our table for dinner. The food was exquisite and the hotel had arranged entertainment so we were enthralled by a troupe of dancers and then entertained by a live band during dessert.

After dinner, people gravitated towards the dance floor as the tables were cleared away. I wasn't quite ready to dance so I stood at the edge of the dance floor sipping on a glass of champagne. Suddenly I felt an arm snake around me and found myself being whisked onto the dance floor. My dance partner had smooth and fluid moves on the dance floor but there was something hauntingly familiar about the way he held me. The self-assured way that he lead me, as if we had been partners before. As the song ended he leant down and whispered in my ear "You didn't think I would let you go so easily did you?" and with a sickening feeling, I realised that Miles was my dance partner. I stood frozen to the spot, shocked to see him there. I had begged him to visit Guyana with me on numerous occasions and now he was here in the worst possible circumstances.

ABOUT THE PUBLISHER

Welcome to the world of RHJ Publishing. Although conceptualised in 2006, the brand was formally launched in May 2016 in tribute to the late Roydon Haigh Josiah.

Our name reflects the rich ancestry of our founders and enables us to share

HIStory and **HER**story

The stories that we share come in all shapes and sizes and we celebrate the eclectic mix of voices and mediums that we use.

We work both formally and informally with writers and creatives to tell their stories and find the best way to share their craft.

We also take great pleasure in working with the next generation of writers by mentoring, supporting and empowering EVERYONE to find their voice.

Our primary distributor is ROI Jelly Ltd, who we work closely with to bring our products to market.

Get involved and have your say:

@RoianneNedd   (Author)

@RHJPublishing (Publisher)

www.facebook.com\ZaviaFraser

Email roijelly@outlook.com for further information

RHJ Publishing is a brand of ROI Jelly Ltd

www.ingramcontent.com/pod-product-compliance
Lightning Source LLC
Chambersburg PA
CBHW071349170626
46811CB00003B/1057